Big Girls Do It
Married

JASINDA WILDER

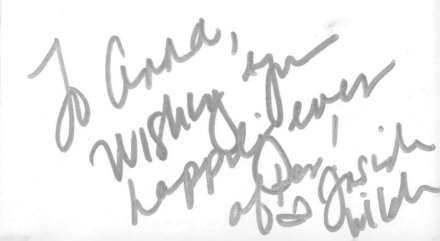

To Anna,
wishing you
happily ever
after
Jasinda
Wilder

This is a work of fiction. Names, characters, places, and incidents are either the product of the author's imagination or are used fictitiously. Any resemblance to actual events, places, organizations, or persons, whether living or dead, is entirely coincidental.

BIG GIRLS DO IT MARRIED

ISBN: 978-0-9882642-5-0
Copyright © 2012 by Jasinda Wilder

To all the awesome ladies of Team Wild,
you rock my socks!

Chapter 1

CHASE PROPOSED TO ME.

Holy shit.

What was I supposed to do? Jeff had proposed to me the day before. Two proposals of marriage in two days. Seriously? Who does this

happen to?

Me, apparently.

I shoved open the door and ran out into the night, sobs ripping from my throat. I heard voices behind me, Jeff's and Chase's. They both called my name, told me to wait.

Then I heard Jeff's voice again, deeper, harder, growling. "Back off, pretty boy. You had your chance." "Who the hell asked you?" Chase, angry.

I stopped, sensing trouble. Jeff had sounded threatening. Chase had sounded equally threatening.

Two proposals, and now the two men were about to fight over me. I'm sure some girls might find that sexy or something, but not me. There's nothing hot about the two men in love with you making each other bloody over you. Two men in love with you is messy, period. Flattering, yes. But it's complicated and difficult, and I don't recommend it.

I turned in time to see Chase push past Jeff, who was trying to keep Chase from coming after me. Jeff shoved Chase, spinning him in the process. A fist flashed, and Chase went down with a grunt, bleeding.

"Stop!" I ran over to them, pushed Jeff away, knelt down beside Chase. Jeff backed away, fists clenched, eyes narrow and angry. "Anna?"

That single word, my name dropping from Jeff's lips, held a thousand questions, a thousand recriminations. I looked up at him. He wasn't just angry at Chase.

"Jeff, I didn't know he would do this. I haven't seen or spoken to him since I left New York." I stood up and met Jeff's eyes. "I promise, I didn't know he'd do this."

"Okay, then." The anger faded from his eyes, but the hardness didn't. "Leave, pretty boy."

Chase stood up, angry. "Fuck you. I'll leave when I want, cowboy. I have a right to talk to her. She doesn't belong to you."

Jeff pushed forward, but I stopped him with a gentle hand to his chest. "Jeff, no. Please. Let me talk to him. Go in, run the shift. I'll be there in a few minutes."

He hesitated, looking from me to Chase and back again. I realized I was the one he didn't entirely trust. "Jeff, please. I'll be fine, I swear. I mean, don't worry, okay? It's not like that."

He grunted, his lip curling in a frown, but he turned on his heel and went back into The Dive.

Chase waited till Jeff was gone and then turned to me, wiping the blood sluicing from his nose on the back of his arm. "Anna, listen, I—" "Chase, what the hell were you thinking?" I turned away from him, because looking at him made my head and my heart and my body all go in different directions. "You can't just show up where I work and propose to me in front of hundreds of people." "It's not hundreds," Chase pointed out. "There's maybe seventy people in there."

"What fucking difference does it make how many people there are, Chase? You embarrassed me!" I turned back to him, my face flushed hot with anger. "Putting me on the spot like that isn't the way to win me back, if that's what you're going for."

"Embarrassed you? I asked you to marry me!"

"Yeah, but I wasn't ready!" I was yelling loudly, but I didn't care at the moment. "You can't just show up after a month of silence and propose, Chase. It doesn't work like that."

Now it was Chase's turn to yell. "I tried for weeks to get a hold of you, Anna! You ran without giving me a chance to explain. I sent a million texts, called and left a million voicemails. You never so much as acknowledged me."

The hurt in his eyes made my heart clench.

"Chase, I can't have this conversation now. I have to work."

He sighed and rubbed his forehead with his knuckles. "Fine. When, then?"

"Tomorrow, lunch. Call me and we'll meet." The hurt on his face turned to hope, forcing me to backtrack. "Look, I'm not agreeing to anything. I'm just saying I'll meet with you and give you a chance to explain. That's *it*. Okay?"

He nodded and stepped into me for a hug, his arms sliding around my waist. I was disoriented for a long moment, feeling the anger and embarrassment and confusion warring with my physical desire for and comfort with him. I managed to push him back and step away.

"Chase, stop." My voice was small; I couldn't meet his eyes. "Stop trying to confuse me."

"I wasn't—"

"I have to go." I turned and walked away without a backward glance.

The bar was buzzing. No one met my eyes or spoke to me. Jeff was setting up the song queue when I got back to the karaoke stage; the glance he shot my way was equal parts worry, anger, and resignation.

I waited until the song was under way, a big blond man doing fair justice to "Crash" by Dave Matthews Band.

"Jeff," I said, leaning close to him, my hand on the back of his shoulder. "I know what that must have seemed like to you. But please, please believe me, I had nothing to do with it. I haven't seen him, texted him, emailed him, called him, nothing, since I left New York."

He shrugged, not quite looking at me. "Okay."

"Goddamn it, Jeff." I picked up a Keno pencil and snapped it between my fingers, toying with the halves. "I need you to believe me. I didn't know he would do that. I didn't want him to."

Jeff blew a long breath out, puffing his cheeks and rolling his shoulders. "All right, Anna. All right." He put his hand on my knee and squeezed lightly. "I'll make the choice to trust you."

I had to tell him I was meeting Chase for lunch tomorrow, but now wasn't the time. It'd have to wait until after we were done working.

The shift dragged on forever. Each song seemed to take an hour, and each performance was worse than the last. Finally we finished, loaded up, and went home, once again not staying for a drink. I could use one, but I'd rather wait until we were home so I could get Jeff relaxed before pissing him off all over again.

We got back to his place, carted the equipment back into his garage, and plopped down on his couch with beer and a bag of pretzels. Jeff sat down and propped his legs up on the coffee table, waiting. I curled up next to him, feet crossed underneath me.

We drank in silence for a few minutes, and then Jeff nudged my thigh with his beer bottle. "You got something to say. Spit it out."

I bit my lip, then let my head flop back onto the couch as I answered. "I told Chase I'd meet him for lunch tomorrow, give him a chance to say his piece." I held up my hand to stall his objections. "I was very clear with him. I told him it wasn't for anything but to give him a chance to explain. Nothing is changing."

"The hell it isn't," Jeff said. "I asked you to *marry* me yesterday, Anna. You said you needed time to think about it. Then pretty boy shows up and asks you, too. What am I supposed to think?"

"His name is Chase," I said. "Not 'pretty boy.' I know you don't like him, and I don't expect you to. But don't be a dick about it, okay?"

"So should I just take the ring back, then?" Jeff asked.

My heart throbbed at the tone in his voice, despair tangled with anger.

"No, Jeff. Please, you're not being fair. I know how this must seem to you—"

"I don't think you do, Anna." Jeff set his beer bottle down and turned on the couch to face me. "I've been in love with you for six years. You know that? This isn't just a sudden thing for me. I've loved you since the very first song we sang together. Remember what it was?"

"'I'll Be' by Edwin McCain."

"Yeah. You acted like you didn't notice I was in love with you, so I didn't push it. I liked being your friend. I liked working with you. I wanted you in my life any way I could get you, even if that meant never saying anything about how I felt." Jeff looked down and scratched at the couch with a fingernail. "I love you, Anna. But I'm not waiting around anymore. You gotta choose."

"You're making this something it's not, Jeff. There's nothing to choose. I love you. I had no idea he was even here. You think that's the kind of proposal I'd like? In public? A complete surprise?"

Jeff shook his head. "He's an idiot. He doesn't know shit about you if he thinks that would work. But that's not the point. I don't think you're over him. I think you still wonder about him, about New York. I saw your face. You hated the shock of it, but the fact that he'd shown up and was doing something to get your attention, that hit you hard."

I couldn't answer for a long time. I stared at the carpet until the pattern wavered.

"Maybe you're right," I said, finally. "What the hell am I supposed to do? I would have been fine if he'd just stayed in New York. I would have wondered every once in a while, but I would've been fine. Now? I don't know."

I was talking to myself more than Jeff, but he answered anyway.

"Well, go and talk to him, then. I'm not gonna say I don't care, 'cause I do. Do what you have to do."

"I'm just meeting him to hear what he has to say. That's it."

"And what if he says he loves you, and he wants you to go to New York with him? What if he kisses you, and begs you, tells you that you were wrong about what you saw? What if he has proof he didn't do anything? What then?"

I couldn't answer. Those questions were banging in my head, too. I shrugged. "I don't know," I whispered. "But…don't leave me, okay? Give me a chance. Please?"

Jeff drained his beer. "Do what you have to do." He stood up and looked down at me sadly. "We'll take things one step at a time."

He poured the suds at the bottom down the drain and set his bottle on the counter, then reached into his shorts pocket. He took out a black ring box and set it on the table, turned without looking at me or the ring, and went into his room.

I sat on the couch, staring at the ring box, drinking my beer and wishing the answer would strike me like lightning. It didn't. I moved to the table and sat down in front of the little black box, but I didn't touch it yet. I set my beer down, wiped my damp fingers on my shirt, and opened the box.

The ring was as breathtaking as it had been the first time I saw it. I lifted the ring out of the box and held it between my finger and thumb. The light refracted on the myriad facets, glinted from the platinum. My eyes burned, my sight wavered, and then a single tear dripped to the glass surface of the table.

What the hell am I supposed to do?

No answer came.

I stared at the ring for a long time, trying to sort out what I felt for Jeff and what I felt for Chase. Sitting there alone, all I could think was that they were both important to me. They both said they loved me. They both wanted me.

Me. *Me.* Anna Devine.

How was I supposed to make this choice?

I couldn't.

I put the ring back, closed the box, and shut off the lights before going into Jeff's—our—bedroom. I lay down next to him, afraid to touch him. Sleep was a long time coming.

Jeff was gone when I woke up. He'd left a note:

Anna,

I need some time. Went to the gym to work out, then to the shooting range with some Army buddies. Just know, whatever happens, I love you. I want you to be happy.

Jeff.

I stared at the note, written in Jeff's all-caps scrawl, tersely worded. Those last six words haunted me: "I want you to be happy." I knew Jeff. I knew what he was saying. He loved me enough to let me make my own choice. He'd made his feelings clear, and that was that. He'd let me go, if that's what I wanted.

It would have been easier in some ways if he'd recriminated with me, fought for me, stayed angry. But that just wasn't Jeff. He would fight for me, though. He'd punched Chase, after all. Although I suspected the punch was more about his own jealousy than protecting me. I hadn't needed protection, after all.

The morning passed slowly. I ended up back at my apartment, which was sans Jamie again. I showered, changed, and tried to figure out what the hell I was going to do. Like the night before, no answers came.

Eventually I texted Chase rather than waiting for him: *Meet me at National Coney Island in Royal Oak in twenty minutes.*

A few minutes passed, then he responded. *K. OMW. See you there.*

I gathered my courage and left.

He was waiting for me. My belly quivered at the sight of him, like it always did. How could it not? He was so beautiful. He'd changed, though. His thick black hair, usually carefully spiked in an intentionally messy way, had been shorn to the scalp. He'd gauged his earlobes, and now had quarter-inch-diameter black plugs. He was wearing a sleeveless T-shirt, and I could see new tattoos spiraling around his left bicep and shoulder. Shaving his head, which I normally found unattractive, brought the sharp planes and angles of his face into high relief and made his eyes stand out, vivid brown so dark it was almost black.

He was tapping a message in a cell phone when I arrived, and so didn't see me until I sat down on the opposite side of the booth.

He started at my appearance. "Shit, you scared me," he said, laughing. "Thanks for coming."

"I don't want you to think my meeting you means I've agreed to anything. It's a courtesy."

He nodded, sipping his Coke. "I get it."

The waitress came and we ordered. When she was gone, Chase took a deep breath and started talking.

"First, you were right about the proposal. I'm sorry, that was kind of a dumb idea, in retrospect. I just—I had to get your attention somehow."

"Well, you have it, for now."

"I guess the most important thing I need you to understand is that I wasn't doing anything with those girls. I know how it looked, but it wasn't like that. They surprised me in the alley, okay? I was out there getting some air after the show, and they cornered me, jumped all over me. You came out as I was telling them I wasn't going to do that with them, and they needed to get off me because I didn't want you to find me in a compromising position and get the wrong idea."

"Which is exactly what you're saying happened."

"Right," Chase said.

Our food came, and we ate in silence for several minutes.

"Here's my question," Chase said. "I don't think the business with those girls was the real reason you ran off on me."

"So what do you think it was?"

"I think you were afraid of falling in love with me. I think you felt things happening and you panicked. The whole wrong timing business just gave you an excuse to run."

"You may be right," I agreed, not looking at him. "But it doesn't matter now."

"How could it not matter? Feelings like that don't just vanish in a month or two, Anna. You still feel something for me. I know you do. I saw it in your face when you first saw me at the bar."

I shrugged. "Maybe there are still feelings there, but I'm with Jeff now. I can't just run off on him again."

"Again?"

"Whatever—"

"No, not whatever, Anna, what'd you—"

"Let it go, Chase," I said, making my voice hard. "Listen, we had a great time in New York. You really showed me things about myself that I needed to see. Thank you for that. You opened my eyes and helped me realize I'm more than just my pants size. I can never repay you for that. But it's not enough to base a relationship on." I swirled the ice in my glass with my straw, staring down at the cubes as they bobbed and clinked in the brown bubbles of the Coke. "And besides that, you're a rising star, Chase. You've got a sick amount of talent. Your band is going to be huge, I promise you. You don't need a girlfriend holding you back."

"How would you be holding me back?" Chase asked.

"I need a man who's going to be faithful. I need someone who'll be there with me. *Here* with me. I don't want to live in New York."

"I'd be faithful—"

"I'm sure you'd mean to be. But when you're famous and girls like that are throwing themselves at you every night, and not just one or two, but dozens every show, eventually, you wouldn't be. You'd give in, and it would make things tough. You don't need a girlfriend. You need the freedom to live the rock star life. I mean, don't do drugs or anything, 'cause that's stupid. But you know what I mean."

He nodded, dipping a fry in cheese and then ranch. "I get what you're saying, and you're right to an extent. But I love you. I'm in love with you. I can't just ignore that."

"Chase...I know where you're going with this." I reached across the table and took his hand in mine. "You can't give up this opportunity. You could be the next huge thing, you know? Like Daughtry or whoever. I was gonna say Nickelback, but everybody hates Nickelback, right? Whatever. The point is, you can't walk away from this. Not for me."

"Then come with me. We're going on tour in a few weeks. A U.S. tour at first, then if everything goes well, a European one."

"You want me to tag along with you on a world tour? And do what? Sit backstage every show? Wait for you on the tour bus?"

"Sure, why not? It could be fun. You'd meet bands, go with me to signings and events and stuff."

"No, Chase. I don't think so. I know you mean well, but that's not a life for me. I'm not meant to be an arm-candy, wait-backstage kind of girlfriend. I want more than that. I *deserve* more than that."

"What are you going to do here, then?" Chase asked. "DJ karaoke for the rest of your life? Have Jeff's kids and be a soccer mom?"

Anger boiled through me. "Fuck you, Chase." I stood up and threw money on the table, turned around, and stomped off.

I'd made it out of the restaurant and to my car when I felt him grab my arm and turn me around. I jerked my arm free. "What if that's what I want? What if I like DJing karaoke? What if I want to marry Jeff and have his kids and be a soccer mom? You have something against soccer moms?"

"No, Anna, that wasn't my point. If that's what you want, then fine, go for it. My point was, you're more talented than that. You've got a great voice. You've got stage presence, and you know how to put on a performance. If you came to New York with me, I could probably score you a meeting with a record exec. You might get a deal, be a singer for real."

My heart stopped. "You could do that?"

"Easy. My producer said you had a stunning voice. He said he'd consider signing you himself."

I had a moment of dreaming: me, alone on a stage, performing; spotlights on me, my name on the marquee.

But then reality butted in.

"Chase, that's not me," I said. "Yeah, sure, the idea of being a singer, recording and touring and all that, it sounds great on paper. But if I did that, when would we ever see each other? The music I'd make isn't like yours. We wouldn't tour together. We wouldn't record together. So we'd have different careers, and wouldn't really be together. So if I'm not with you, why would I leave? It just doesn't compute, in my mind. I guess what it comes down to, really, is that I don't have a desire to be famous. I just…I don't know what I *do* want for my future exactly, but a life of paparazzi and magazine articles and whatever, that's not me."

Chase put his back to the car and pinched the bridge of his nose. "You're really dead set against letting this work, aren't you?" He sighed. "Fine. I guess I'll see you around."

"God, Chase. It's not that I'm against it, it's just that I don't see it working out with us."

"You're not even willing to try?"

"I don't know."

Chase's eyes bored into me. I felt the brunt of his emotions hitting me, his hope and his love and his fear. He really did love me. "You're afraid, Anna. You're afraid I don't really love you, or that I can't be faithful while I'm on tour. But you do love me. Or at least, you *could*, if you'd let yourself."

"You're right, Chase. Is that what you want to hear? Yeah, I left because I was falling in love, and it scared me. But it wasn't you, or the idea of being in love with you that had me panicking. Some of the things that happened in New York bothered me, and I'm not talking about seeing you with the girls. It was...I don't know how to put it. It wasn't me. It was fun, and I enjoyed it, but I don't think it was things I'd do normally. You have a way of bringing out the wildness in me, and I'm not sure I'm comfortable with that."

"You're talking about the bathroom thing."

"That's part of it, yes."

"It doesn't have to be like that—"

"Chase, stop. If that's the thing you like, then you should be free to do it. I'm just not sure that's the scene I'm into. I tried it, and...I don't know. The sex was great, but being walked in on, being seen? Sex is private to me, I guess. Sex is always great with you. But I need a relationship that's not just sex."

Chase looked hurt. "You think our relationship is just about sex?"

"I think that's a big part of it. I'm intensely attracted to you. Every time I see you I get all quivery inside. You turn me on just by being you. You're out of my league in a major way. I love having sex with you. It's seriously incredible. But there's got to be more. We barely know each other. I'm not sure what we have in common, long term." I had to physically restrain myself from touching him to comfort him, he looked so forlorn. "And I *really* want long term."

"But I can do long term. I can."

"I'm not doubting that. I'm doubting whether you can do long term with *me*."

Chase turned away from me. "I can't win this argument, can I?"

"It's not an argument," I said, softly.

"Then what is it? Me, begging?" He shook his head, then turned back to me, put his hands on my waist above the swell of my hips. "Anna, I love you. I don't know what else I can say or do to convince you. I'll say it once more. Please, be with me."

My throat felt thick. "Chase, I—I don't know. I don't think I can. If I leave Jeff, he'll be heartbroken. I can't do that again."

"What about me? If you turn me down, *I'll* be heartbroken. Or don't you care about that?"

I tried desperately to pull away from his touch, but I couldn't. "Of course I care, Chase. No matter what I do, someone gets hurt. Please, don't make this harder than it has to be."

Chase's eyes narrowed. "It doesn't have to be hard. Just come with me. Jeff is a big boy. He can deal. Just come with me. I can make you happy. You know I can."

Something in my belly and below it trembled and turned to liquid. The heat in his eyes told me exactly what Chase had in mind when he said he could make me happy. I knew he was right. He could make me happy. My entire body shook with raw, potent desire. For a moment all I could think was how badly I wanted to drag him back to my apartment and rip his clothes off, let him make me happy.

I wrenched myself out of his grip. "No. Not like this."

Chase watched with a tight, pained expression. I got in my car, started it, and backed out. He stopped me with a palm slapping against my window.

I stopped and rolled my window down. "What do you want now, Chase?" Exasperation was rife in my voice.

He reached into his pants pocket and pulled out a black box.

Goddamn it. I was starting to hate those little boxes.

"Chase, for god's sake—"

"Just listen, damn it." He reached through the window and put the box, closed, on my lap. "Take it. Think about it. I love you. I'll give up being a rockstar to be with you. I'll stay here. I'll go wherever you want. I'll even sell my bike and drive a minivan if that's what you want. I just want you."

And then he was gone, leaving me trembling and hearing his words.

I managed to make it home before collapsing into sobs. Even in the midst of my confused, heartaching tears, it felt weird to be in my own bed in my apartment. I'd spent so much time over the last few weeks at Jeff's house that my place was starting to feel less and less like home. Jeff was home. I managed to get my bawling under control and lay on my bed, staring at my room. This small space had once been my haven. I'd come here after work, half-drunk and lonely and horny, and I'd read a book or a magazine, or watch TV on the tiny set Jamie had given me on my birthday.

I was comfortable here. I knew where everything was, where everything belonged. The pile of clothes in the corner by the dresser wasn't just a pile of clothes. It was a specifically sorted pile of clothes; shirts were on top, pants, shorts, and skirts on bottom. The magazines stacked on top of the dresser were piled in order of how much I liked each issue. The bra hanging on the doorknob was clean, the one hanging in the bathroom was dirty.

It looked like a mess to a casual observer, but it was my mess, and it was an organized mess.

Now, after the military cleanliness of Jeff's place, it just looked messy. Jeff would shoot me irritated glances if I left my clothes on the floor. He wouldn't get mad or yell at me—he'd just pick it up and make me feel guilty with a few calculated glances. Now, lying in my bed, looking at the piles of crap, I realized I didn't feel comfortable here anymore. It had felt like my nest before spending so much time at Jeff's.

I wanted to be back at Jeff's. What did that mean? Did it mean I loved him more than Chase? I hadn't really liked being at Chase's place. It was a room in a house he shared with his band. It was clean enough, nice enough, but it just hadn't felt like home.

Jeff's house was home. Jeff was home.

But Chase…he was exciting. He made me dizzy with desire, pure lust, unadulterated greed for his body. He was a rockstar. He'd be famous. I could be famous just for being his girlfriend.

Jamie wouldn't hesitate. The chance to be with a real live rockstar, an up-and-coming player on the music scene, that wasn't an opportunity to pass up. Especially not when the sex was so mind-blowing.

I found myself out of bed and cleaning up as I thought. My bed got made, the clothes stacked on it folded, put away. Dirty laundry was set outside my door to wash, magazines and books were put away on the bookshelf opposite my bed. I even vacuumed.

None of this, however, got me any closer to knowing what to do.

I felt better about my room, and was able to actually relax without feeling claustrophobic. I also knew if Jeff came over, he'd be comfortable. He'd tried coming over once, but after that one visit, he'd never suggested coming back. It may have had something to do with the loud and vocal sex noises coming from Jamie's room, but my mess was the largest part of it, even if he'd never said anything.

Chase wouldn't have minded. He'd have cleared a path to the bed, added our clothes to the mess, and turned his attention to my body.

Was that something to base a decision on? Suddenly, every little factor and facet of the two men was brought into focus. Jeff was clean, neat, organized, methodical. He was steady, stable. Not predictable, because he'd shown a capacity for constantly surprising me. But I could always depend on him.

Even now, stewing in my room, I knew I could expect to hear from him soon. He'd get tired of waiting and wonder where I was. He'd want to know what I was doing, even if it was just to make sure I was safe.

Was Chase dependable? My gut told me he'd be there if I needed him. He really would give up his rising career in music if I told him that was the price to be with me. He'd turn his back on it all and stay here with me. He'd play local gigs, maybe start DJing with me. He'd give me what I wanted. But...he'd always wonder what could have been if he'd followed his dreams, stuck with the career rather than the girl. Would he resent me?

God, my head was spinning. They were two totally different men, both amazing in their own ways. They were both claiming to be in love with me, and I was faced with the choice between them. This was the stuff of Regency romance books: The plucky and intrepid and oh-so-charming heroine was presented with the impossible task of choosing between the wealthy nobleman offering her a comfortable future and the poor but handsome and completely devoted peasant who loved her unconditionally. Yeah, that was me. Except this was my life. No one was writing this story. I had to make the choice and live with the consequences.

I knew one thing: I'd hurt one of them, whomever I chose, and I'd always wonder in part of my mind what life would have been like if I'd chosen the other.

The buzzer jolted me out of my thoughts. I buzzed the person through without checking to see who it was. I opened the door to see Jeff lifting his fist to knock.

"You *are* here," he said by way of greeting. He didn't move to come in.

"Of course. Where else would I be?"

He frowned. "Gone. New York with pretty— with Chase. You weren't at home—I mean, at my house, so I wasn't sure where you'd be."

I took his arm and pulled him in, shutting the door behind him. "I talked with Chase and then came here. I needed to think." I flopped down on the couch and stared at the signed Bon Jovi poster of Jamie's hung over the TV. "I'm confused, Jeff."

He sat down next to me and stretched his arm out behind my head. I nestled into the hollow of his arm automatically. I don't think either of us realized I was doing it until he had his arm wrapped around me.

"Confused about what?" Jeff asked.

"Everything," I said. "Talking to him just made things worse."

"Could have told you that before you went," Jeff remarked.

"Yeah, and if you had, I would have gone anyway."

"True," Jeff chuckled. "You're stubborn like that."

"I just don't know what to do. You're both so different. But you both claim to love me." I glanced up at Jeff to see him flinch. "Sorry, I guess it's not fair to you to talk about this with you."

"Who else are you gonna talk to about it? I'm still your friend, Anna. That ain't ever gonna change."

"But you're part of the problem." I sighed. "I didn't mean that. You're not a problem. The situation is a problem, and it's my own fault."

"I know what you meant. But if you need to talk, then talk."

"I just don't know what to do."

"You already said that," Jeff pointed out. "Break it down for me like I'm not one of the choices in front of you."

"You both claim to love me. That by itself is hard to swallow. Just a couple months ago I was lonely and depressed. I had you and Jamie, and that was about it. I didn't think I'd ever find anyone to love me, and I hadn't had sex in months and didn't feel beautiful." I pulled my hair out of its ponytail and ran my fingers through it. "Now, everything is different.

"Honestly, a lot of the reason I've begun to realize I'm beautiful is due to Chase. I know you don't want to hear that, but it's true. He started it all. He pursued me, and he made me see myself through his eyes, to a degree. He wanted me. I hadn't felt wanted in…well, ever."

"I wanted you," Jeff said, his voice quiet.

"Yeah, but you didn't do anything about it, Jeff. I didn't know you loved me. I thought it was a crush. You let me pretend it wasn't there for six years."

"I didn't think you wanted me back."

"Would you have ever made a move on your own?" I asked.

"I don't know. Maybe. Maybe not. I wish now I had made a move sooner."

"Me, too." I ran my fingers across Jeff's cheek. "You make me feel beautiful. My point about Chase is that he got me thinking about myself in a different way. I wouldn't have ever had the courage to try anything with you if it hadn't been for him."

"Well, I guess I owe him some thanks, then."

"Me, too," I said. "In a big way."

Jeff got up and went to the bathroom; when he came back he smirked at me. "Your room looks different. Cleaner."

I shrugged. "Your house is always so clean. I've spent so much time there that now my room seems nasty. I couldn't relax until I'd cleaned it up."

Jeff grinned. "Well, glad I'm instilling some good habits in you at least. It was kinda gross the last time I was here."

I slapped his arm. "Gee, thanks, asshole."

He laughed. "Hey, you know what I meant." He scrubbed the smile from his face with his palm. "So you went to talk to Chase, and it made things worse. Why, though? I thought you were just going to hear him out."

"Yeah, well...I guess the problem is I didn't ever really believe he'd done anything awful. It was an excuse. I was feeling things for him that scared me. Plus, I had you on my mind, and I knew I felt things for you, too, and that scared me even more. Like I said when I came back, I felt like I was cheating on you with him, and seeing him with those groupies just made it easier to run. I think I was hoping he'd let me go and this problem I'm having now would be avoided."

"No such luck."

"No," I agreed. "No such luck. And now I've got both of you saying you love me, and I have feelings for both of you, but they're completely different feelings."

"And you don't know what to do," Jeff said.

"Nope."

He blew a long breath out between his teeth. "Well, I can't make the choice for you, obviously. And you know what I want. I want you, I want you to pick me. I think I'm best for you. I think I understand you. I think I can give you what you want and need. I think Chase is exciting and fun, and I'm sure he's talented and going places and all that. But I don't think he's right for you. He may be faithful to you if you pick him and go with him. I can't say he's a bad person. I don't know him well enough to make that call. Maybe he's great. Maybe you'd have the best happily ever after with him. Maybe. But I don't think so." He slid off the couch and knelt in front of me, positioned himself between my knees so our faces were level, within kissing distance. "I love you, Anna. I'll love you forever. I'm being completely honest here when I say I want you to be with me instead of him. But more than anything else, I want you to be happy. No matter what. If you think he's the best choice for you, for your life, then go with him and be happy. I let you go to New York without fighting because I knew you'd always wonder if you didn't, and because I could tell nothing I said would change your mind. I didn't want you to go. But you did, and here we are."

I shook my head. "God, Jeff. That really doesn't help." A sob bubbled out past my lips.

"I didn't say I could help. I said I'd listen. I said you could talk to me about what was bugging you. I can't be anything but honest about what I want, and I can't be objective, either."

"Well, what fucking good are you, then?" I asked. "Kidding. That's the problem, though. You're my best friend, aside from Jamie, and usually you'd help me sort through this."

"Where is Jamie, anyway? Why can't she talk to you about it?"

I shrugged. "I don't know where she is. And I don't think she'd be objective, either. Her taste in men is...different from mine. She has her own issues. I just don't think she'd be able to help me. No one can." Another sob whimpered from me, this one more hysterical.

I was trying to keep it together, but I couldn't, quite. My shoulders shook and my eyes burned. I didn't want to cry.

Jeff didn't have an answer for that. He moved up onto the couch next to me and drew me onto his lap. "Just breathe, Anna. It's going to be okay. It's a shitty thing to have to choose, and I can't say I know how you feel, 'cause I don't. But remember, we're both adults, okay? Yeah, the fact is, one of us will be hurt when you choose the other. But it won't be the end of the world. I'd be heartbroken, and it'd be real long fucking time before I cared for anyone else like I do you, but I'd be okay, in time. I don't know Chase, but I don't imagine he'd flip out off the deep end, either. Hurt heals, Anna. Choosing sucks. Pain sucks. Hurting someone you care about sucks, but that's life. Life hurts. Sometimes we're faced with a shitty fucking choice that leaves everyone involved hurt somehow. All you can do is make the right choice for you and move on."

He put his forefinger under my chin and lifted my face to his. I blinked hard, sniffed back tears, and bit my lip to keep from bursting apart. Jeff's dark eyes were soft and tender and compassionate.

His body was a hard, strong shelter around me. It didn't fix my problem, but with his arms around me, I felt loved, I felt able to keep breathing despite the crushing pressure on my chest.

He kissed me, a slow, feather-soft touch of his lips to mine. "Quit holding it in. You don't have to be strong all the time. You're upset. It's okay to feel it."

His palm rubbed my back, and his fingers brushed tendrils of hair away from my eyes and traced the line of my jaw. I held it in a moment longer, my body trembling with the effort. It began as a single tear down my cheek, then a second. I sniffed, tried to breathe deep enough to hold on to my composure. A sob wrenched my gut, and then another, and then I was wracked by shuddering sobs, a veil of tears obscuring my vision. I was lost then, carried away and helpless. Jeff was my anchor, the only solid thing in my world.

He held me, wiped the tears away, used the hem of his shirt to clean my face.

"I can't do it," I said, when I had enough breath to speak. "I just want to run away from both of you. I can't hurt you. I can't hurt him. There's no right choice." I hiccuped. "I need a cupcake."

Jeff kissed my forehead, then each cheek, and then, last, my lips. "Don't worry about right or wrong. Just worry about what's best for you."

"But I don't *know* what's best for me!"

He kissed my lips again to quiet me, and this time he kept kissing. The sweet, familiar taste of his lips swept me away, his body beneath mine cradled me close and comforted me, and his hands ghosting over my curves pushed thoughts to the background.

Distraction was welcome. A fragmentary thought flitted through my head: *This is only going to confuse me further, later.* But I didn't care. Kissing Jeff was all that was right in my life. My tears subsided and my sobs quieted and my confusion drifted to the background, all subsumed beneath the storm of need for Jeff.

I moaned as his tongue swept into my mouth, and then twisted on his lap so I was facing him, my knees digging down into the crack between couch back and cushion. This was all I needed.

Desire erupted within me, gouging all thoughts from my mind. All I knew was Jeff's mouth, his cock hardening beneath me, his hands on my waist and slipping upward to cup my breasts. I arched my chest into his hands, dragged my fingers through his close-cropped hair and down his sides. My fingers caught the bottom of his shirt, and I lifted it up over his head.

He broke the kiss and pulled back, searching my eyes. "I don't want to make anything harder for you," he said.

I stood up, his shirt balled in my fist, and led him by the hand into my room, closing the door behind us.

He stood uncertainly with his back to the door. "Anna, I don't wanna confuse you—"

I peeled my shirt over my head, unhooked my bra, and then took a step closer to Jeff. He backed up, his hands reaching for me even as he tried to protest. He bumped against the door, and I crushed myself against him.

"Shut up and make love to me, Jeff. I know it's not gonna fix anything, but I need it. I need you. Please."

I popped the button on my jeans and shimmied out of them, then turned my hands to Jeff, tracing the heavy muscles of his chest and the broad, hard bulge of his belly. He ran his hands down my arms, his eyes raking over my body, hungry, burning with lust and shimmering with love. I pressed a kiss to his shoulder, then his pectoral muscle. He thumped his head against the wooden door, rumbling in his chest as I opened his pants and shoved them down.

His thick, hot, hard cock filled my hands, the veins pulsing against my palms, his sack tightening as I cupped it. I ran my hands up and down his length, murmuring in pleasure as I kissed his chest, then his stomach, sliding to my knees in front of him and caressing the cool curve of his ass.

He caught at my shoulders as I knelt, bent to lift me up. I glanced up at him, took his hands in mine, and tangled our fingers. Breaking my gaze away from his, I lowered my mouth to his cock, wrapped my lips around the tip, and carved circles around his crown with my tongue.

"Anna," he groaned.

I wasn't sure if it was a protest or a sound of pleasure. Both, probably. I took him deeper, let him bump against the back of my throat and then backed off. His hands tightened on mine, refusing to let go. I licked his length from base to tip, then swirled my tongue around him, tasting him, teasing him. He moaned again, and I took him deep into my mouth once more, opening the back of my throat until I couldn't take any more.

"God, what are you doing to me?" Jeff asked.

I spat him out and smiled at him. He used the momentary distraction to pull me to my feet. His lips met mine and his hands gripped my hips, pulling our bodies together, crushing his cock between us.

"Anna—" he began, but I silenced him with my mouth, as he had me.

I pushed away from him, lay down on my bed, feet drawn up, knees apart, waiting. Jeff took a step toward me, then another. I cupped a breast in one hand and skimmed my fingers down my belly to my cleft.

Jeff's hands clenched into fists and released, and then I saw the last of his indecision fade away. His lips curled into a sensual smile, and he crawled onto the bed. He prowled toward me, his head going between my knees, his eyes locked onto mine across the expanse of my body, and then lowered between my thighs. I felt a tremble of anticipation waver in the muscles of my legs and belly, gushing through my pussy as a wave of heat and wet desire.

My knees fell apart as his tongue ran up the inside of one thigh, my back arching and my fingers tangling in his hair. I had no thoughts, no mind, no problems, no past or future when he touched me this way, when he kissed my most sensitive and intimate flesh. His fingers touched my folds, found them wet and slid in. His tongue lapped against my lips, then dipped in between them as his fingers curled up as they drew out. I moaned, gasped, whispered his name, pressed his head closer to me. His tongue searched up along the cleft of my labia, found the aching nub of my clit and circled around it, drawing my hips up and my back into a convex bow shape. He knew exactly how to draw the whimpers from me, how to touch me and give me the most pleasure. This was all I needed, all the answers I could ever find, here with him, alone and naked and vulnerable.

Slow swipes around my clit, careful slips of his finger against my G-spot, were replaced by swifter licks and more insistent sliding in and out. I moved my hips into him, whispering his name as climax boiled through me. At the moment of orgasm, my body wracked with shuddering waves, Jeff slid up and drove into me, piercing me in one smooth motion, gliding deep. I shrieked and curled into him, clutching his heavy, hard body against mine, wrapping my legs around his waist and crushing our hips together.

Jeff moaned into my mouth, his thrusts long and slow. His hand cupped my breast, hefted it and squeezed it, and then his fingers rolled my nipple until I shuddered, an aftershock turning into a full-blown orgasm, each thrust of his hips now driving me to further heights of desperate orgasming desire.

I couldn't get him deep enough, couldn't feel his body far enough inside me, pressed hard enough against me. I bit his shoulder as I continued to come, thrusting madly against his measured strokes.

"Harder, Jeff. Harder, please!" I said, each word a whimpered plea.

He answered me with his body rather than words, crashing his cock deeper into me, arching his back and lifting my breast to take a nipple into his mouth. He nipped gently, just hard enough to make me jerk in surprise and come with a curse.

Jeff's motions became ragged and arrhythmic, no longer slow, measured thrusts into me but hard and fast and deep. He cupped the back of my head and lifted me up into a kiss, biting my lower lip as he came, a quick hard pulse of hips against hips and a flood of hot seed inside me. Feeling him come drove me to climax yet again, this one harder than all the rest, curving my body into a spasm of ecstasy.

"Oh, god, Jeff, yes, don't stop," I moaned, feeling the climax drawing out as he continued to thrust, riding the waves of pleasure.

I held him close, feeling him quiver within me, still hard and still pushing deep and pulling out. He kissed me again, kissed me hard and thrust deep.

I felt him softening and pushed him to his side, curling against his chest. He kissed the top of my head, lifted my chin to kiss my lips.

"I love you, Anna, no matter what," Jeff whispered. "I'll always love you. Only you."

Something sharp and hot and bone-deep shifted in my soul. "I love you, too, Jeff. You're my best friend. I don't know what I'd do without you."

In that moment, satisfied in my heart, mind, body, and soul—if only for a fraction of time—I thought I knew what I wanted. If I could have stayed there in that moment forever, I wouldn't have had to make a choice. I nestled close to him, as close as two bodies could be, and wished with all my being to stay there like that forever.

Jeff didn't ruin the moment with further words. He only held me, and left the silence full of our words of love. Decisions could wait. Right then, there was only him and me.

Daylight came, and with it knowledge of Jeff's body spooned behind me, his palm splayed across my belly and his other arm wedged between us. His morning erection was a hard rod against my ass, but his breathing was slow and deep, soft snores telling me he was still asleep. I'd woken with him like this before. It was one of my favorite things, honestly. Early morning light filtered through the window, the air beyond the blankets wrapped beneath our chins was cold, and the warmth of our naked bodies comforting and familiar.

I tangled my fingers in Jeff's hand and moved it to cup my breast, then slipped my fingers down to my pussy. I didn't often touch myself, not anymore. Jeff's hand tightened on my breast as I circled my clit, letting moans whisper past my lips as I spread damp heat through myself with slow-moving fingers. When I began to near climax, I lifted my leg, reached behind me to guide Jeff's stiff cock to my moist entrance. With a sigh of pleasure, I drove him into me, moving my hips in slow flutters on his hard shaft.

I felt his breathing change, felt his body begin to move in time with mine. His fingers on my breast flattened as he stretched, groaning, thrusting into me as he arched his back.

"Goddamn, what a way to wake up," Jeff said, his voice sleep-muzzy.

I tilted my neck back to kiss his jaw, gyrating my hips into his. He moaned, cupping my face in his broad, callused palm, then ran his hand down my throat, pausing to dip in the hollow between throat and chest. Farther down then, to the expanse of skin above my breasts, down between the gravity-pulled flesh, palm spreading to lift a breast, rolling the nipple with gentle, piercing pressure, then resuming the southward journey across the ivory plain of my belly, up the gentle mound of my pudendum. He thrust slowly as he touched me, making love to me with his hand, his lips pressed against the back of my neck.

He rolled with me, pulled me to lie on top of him, back to front, his body pillowing me, his manhood impaling me deep, deep, my knees drawn up between his. His breath huffed in my ear, my name whispered on his lips, and now both his hands roamed my flesh, held my breasts aloft and cupped them and pinched them and paid homage to them, and then his hands curved down my sides to the swelling rise of my hips and to the round muscle of my thighs and inward, to my pussy. He slid into me with a roll of his hips; I lifted my head and craned my neck to watch as he pulled out and pulsed back in, his slick length pistoning into me, his fingers delving into the shallow cup around my clit.

I fell back onto him with a shrieked sigh, feeling a spear of fire shoot through me. His fingers rolled my nipple, the left one, the more sensitive one, and his fingers traced around my throbbing clit in alternating fast-slow, rough-soft circles. I writhed on top of him, my body gone haywire and out my control, my hands gripping his head and clutching at his hands and clawing at his hips.

"Anna, Anna," Jeff said, a note of pleading in his desperation-rough voice, "I love you so fucking much, Anna. You are so beautiful, so amazing."

The utter vulnerability in his voice shredded my heart. I couldn't stop moving, not with climax rocking through me. I couldn't deny the raw love in his words, in his touch. I wanted to deny it. It scared me. I didn't know what to do with it.

Even as I continued to come apart on top of him, I felt fear ripping at me. I didn't know if I could love him as he loved me. He had no doubts, no hesitation, no reason to hold back. He was in love with me, and he'd owned it.

"Jeff..." His name was all I could push past trembling lips.

He pushed into me, his long middle finger curling down and in to find my G-spot at the very moment I peaked in climax, driving me to scream his name, unable to control even the volume of my voice. I'm sure every neighbor within three apartments heard me, and I didn't care. Not then, at least.

He came as I screamed, clutching both of my breasts and holding tight with primal strength, bellowing and thrashing into me, lifting me high with his thrusting hips. I wrapped my arm behind his head and rode him as he bucked into me, the other hand gripping his thigh with clawed fingers.

He stilled, and I lay back on top of him, panting. After a moment, I rolled off him, carefully pulling him out of my cleft.

"Holy shit," Jeff said. "I haven't even had my coffee yet."

I laughed. "I woke up and you had a hard-on. Seemed a shame to let such a beautiful erection go to waste."

He laughed with me, but I noticed the humor didn't quite reach his eyes. There was sadness lurking in his deep brown eyes, something hard and hollow. He kissed me, a quiet touch of lips, and then left the bed. He cracked my bedroom door and peered out, looking for Jamie, seemed satisfied that she wasn't around, and then disappeared into the bathroom. I heard the shower start, and I was alone in my room with my thoughts.

Now that I didn't have Jeff to distract me, an overwhelming wave of pain rolled through me. Jeff loved me so completely. How could I walk away from that? He expected me to, that much was clear from the sadness in his eyes. He'd tried to hide it, and I don't think anyone else would have seen it but me. It was buried deep. It was in the shine of his eyes, the way his glances lingered on me, in the wrinkles at the corners, in the downward tilt of his mouth seen only for a moment before he forced a smile on his lips.

I glanced at the floor, at the pile of clothes. Jeff's jeans sat on top, and I could make out a square bulge in one of his pockets. I knew what it would be even as I lifted the heavy denim, jingling with change and keys. I dug in the pocket, found the small soft black velvet box. When I opened it, the diamond glittered in the early morning sunlight.

The ring was so beautiful. It was simple, not extravagant or gaudy. Just a band of platinum with a single stone, elegantly cut. Like any girl, I'd always loved diamonds, always dreamed of wearing them. I knew what made an expensive ring; this had cost Jeff a *lot* of money. He wasn't a rich man, not by any stretch of the imagination. He drove a truck he'd bought five years ago, and he took immaculate care of it, kept it clean, tuned the engine himself once a month. His house was paid for, I was pretty sure. He had some money saved from his time in the Army, but his only income was DJing. He didn't have the kind of money lying around that he could just suddenly decide to buy a ring as pricey as this one.

He'd never asked me my ring size. I couldn't help wondering if it would fit. It wasn't a conscious decision, but I found myself lifting the ring from the slit in the box, angling it to catch the light, then slipping it onto the ring finger of my left hand.

It fit perfectly.

My throat closed up at the sight of Jeff's ring on my finger, knowing he'd bought it with me in mind. He'd spent a huge chunk of his savings on this piece of metal and mineral.

He wanted to marry me. He wanted to spend every single day for the rest of his life with me. Both of us came from broken homes, parents who had divorced and left distrust and pain in the wake of their ruined marriages. One of the things Jeff and I had talked about, in the long soft hours of afterglow, was how if either of us ever married, it would be once, forever.

When you grow up shuffling between Mom's house and Dad's house as I did—watching them fight in the kitchen every evening in the years before the split, watching them snipe at each other every holiday, every time they ended up face to face with me in the middle—you end up hating the thought of divorce, hating the thought of making so poor a choice of husband that you hate him after a few short years of vicious arguments and tumultuous makeup sex.

I stared at Jeff's ring on my finger, thinking for the first time in many, many years about my parents. They'd split when I was nine, and they'd had me less than a year after they were married. I'd long suspected I was the reason they'd married. The math added up, to my adult brain. If I turned nine the year they celebrated their ninth anniversary, that pretty clearly pointed to a shotgun wedding. I knew both sets of grandparents well enough to be fairly certain if Mom had turned up pregnant at twenty, they'd have pushed my parents into a rush wedding.

Brian and Laura Devine hadn't been a happy couple. They were attracted to each other, that much was clear to me even at a young age. They were always touching each other. I'd heard them having sex all too often as a child, and had walked in on them more than once. They'd just yelled at me to get out, and then told me to mind my own business when I asked what they'd been doing. I learned quickly, without "the talk," what they were doing. As often as they had sex, they fought even more. I fell asleep more nights than not with the sound of their yelling voices. I never knew what they fought about, and I still don't. I can guess, now, though: everything. They were not a good match. They were both stubborn and headstrong and quick-tempered, passionate and physical. Neither was ever willing to compromise, or listen to the other side.

They were attracted to each other, and I understand now as an adult that they had an intense sexual relationship, but it was never enough to make the relationship work long-term.

I layered my understanding of my parents' relationship over top of my relationship with Jeff. Did we have a relationship outside of sex? I didn't even have to ask that question. We had been close friends and partners for years before we ever had sex together. I could assess Jeff's mood just by looking at him. I could almost hear his thoughts sometimes. I felt myself wondering what our relationship would be like in ten years, or twenty. If I felt now, after a few weeks of being with him, that I knew him inside and out, what would it be like in twenty years?

The thought set my hands to trembling.

I didn't want to be like my parents had been. I knew Jeff felt the same way. His dad had walked out on Jeff and his mom and brother when Jeff was eleven. No warning, no reasons, no note. Just packed a suitcase and walked out, in the middle of family dinner. Jeff hadn't ever seen him again, or heard from him. His mother hadn't remarried, Jeff said.

All this bubbled in my head as I gazed at my left hand with the spot of silver brilliance on the ring finger.

"Does it fit?" Jeff's voice startled me.

I tried to wiggle the ring off quickly, as if ashamed to be wearing it. Jeff knelt in front of me and laid his hand over mine. His eyes drilled into mine.

"Does the ring fit?" he asked again.

I nodded. "It fits perfectly," I said, my voice breaking into a whisper at the end. "It's beautiful, Jeff."

Jeff nodded. "It's beautiful, like you." He took my left hand in his right, adjusted the ring with his thumb, staring at it rather than at me. "If you're wearing it, does that mean...?" He trailed off, as if giving voice to his hope would banish it from coming true.

"I don't know. Yes. I don't know."

Jeff laughed. "Sounds like you're still confused."

I shrugged. We were both staring at the ring on my finger rather than meeting gazes.

"I was just looking at it," I said. "I was hoping looking at the ring would, like...I don't know, provide an answer or something. I ended up thinking about Mom and Dad."

He frowned, knowing how seldom I thought about my parents. "Your folks? Why'd you think of them?"

I drew a long breath and let it out. "I don't know, really. I just did. They were so unhappy together. They had great sex, but that was the extent of their relationship."

"It's kind of weird that you know that about your parents," Jeff said, making a face of disgust.

"That's how they were. I saw them together more than once. I heard them all the time." I hesitated, then let my thoughts pour out to Jeff. "I don't want to be like them. I don't want to have a marriage based on that. I don't want to be married if it's not going to last. I'd always thought I'd never get married, then Bruce happened. Fucking Bruce. I was only with him because I thought he was all I could get. I can't believe I wasted so many years of my life on him. After I broke up with him, I swore I'd never get married."

"He was an asshole," Jeff said. "I never liked him. I never thought he was good enough for you."

I let out a mirthless laugh. "God, Jeff, you don't know the half of it. He was beyond asshole and into some other territory. There aren't words for how fucking awful he was to me. He never hit me, but he was verbally abusive. He'd call me names. Tell me I was fat. I needed to lose weight so he'd be more attracted to me. Told me I was only good for one thing, and I wasn't even that good at it."

Jeff rocked back on his heels, the towel wrapped around his waist coming loose. "Are you serious? He said that to you?"

"All the time."

"I never knew." Jeff seemed shocked, hurt, insulted.

"No one did," I whispered. "I never let on to anyone. I thought it was all I was worth. All

I deserved. I thought for a long time my parents had split because of me. I know differently now, of course. I thought guys like Bruce were the normal way for guys to treat girls. He was my first, you know? My first real boyfriend, and I thought I loved him."

Jeff moved to sit on the bed next to me. "Anna, I—"

"It doesn't matter now, Jeff. I'm fine. I learned after I left him that I didn't need to take that shit. I deserved better. Well, I learned that the hard way, in some ways. But I learned it. My point is, after him I never wanted to get married. He'd assumed we'd get married and I'd stay home and have his kids and fuck him whenever he wanted and cook his dinners. That's what he told me. It's why I left him, ultimately. He told me he was gonna buy me a ring and we'd get married the next summer and proceeded to explain what he expected of me." I laughed. "It's funny, though. I tolerated his verbal abuse for, like, three years, day in and day out. I took it, and thought it was fine. I thought it was worth it for the times he was good to me, when he'd buy me nice things and take me to nice dinners and stuff. But when he told me he expected me to cook for him and wash his fucking underwear, I lost it. I told myself I'd never tie myself to a guy, after that."

Jeff shook his head in disbelief. "Anna, listen, that's not what I—"

"I know, Jeff," I said. "I know that's not what you expect. I love you. I know you better than that."

"So what does that mean for us?" Jeff hesitated, then said, "What does that mean for what I—for… god, I can't even say it."

"I don't know. I love you. I can't imagine anyone else knowing me the way you do. But get married? It's such a scary thought, Jeff. I don't know why. I trust you. I know you. I like our relationship. I don't want it to change."

Jeff let the silence hang for a long time.

"Anna, listen. I know what you're afraid of. Like you said, you don't want our relationship to change. But you gotta understand something. Marriage isn't some magical thing. Putting the rings on and saying 'I do' doesn't make the marriage. It doesn't mean you'll love each other any better. All that comes from what you've already got. Marriage only means as much as you make of it. To your parents, it was something expected of them. It was a burden, a rope tying them together. They were meant to be…I don't know, ships in the night, or something. Passing by each other, a few nights of good times, then going on their way. But it doesn't always work like that. Sometimes a night of pleasure turns into a child, and a family that wasn't meant to be. I think that's how it was with my mom and dad. He didn't love her. He stayed with her as long as he could, but she wasn't enough. Jim and I weren't enough."

He took my chin in his fingers and forced my gaze to his. "But you and I, we've got more. You know we do. I told you I loved you enough to let you go. I do, and I mean that, but don't think I'll let you go easily, and don't think I'd ever get over it. You are what I want in life, Anna." He leaned in to kiss me, soft, slow, and sweet. "The time I've spent with you is better than anything I've ever known. I don't want it to ever end."

A tear carved a tickling line down my cheek, caught at the corner of my mouth by Jeff's lips. I slid my fingers around the back of his neck as he kissed my jaw, the corner of my lips, my cheekbones, my throat. My heart hammered in my chest, as if anticipating something my mind wasn't aware of yet.

Words came out of my mouth, and I heard them as if from someone else. "I'll marry you, Jeff."

When I heard myself say it, tears flowed, and I felt the meaning hit me. I did want to marry him. Only him.

Jeff's lips froze on my skin between my breasts. "What?" He straightened, fear of having misheard warring with joy in his eyes. "What did you just say?"

I took his face in my hands. "I said I will marry you. Yes. Yes. I love you, and I want to marry you."

I kissed his lips, long and deep. "I don't want it to ever end, either."

"It doesn't have to," Jeff said, breaking the kiss just long enough to speak.

His fingers tangled with mine, and I felt the ring on my finger as a warm weight. It felt right, there on my finger. I've never been much for jewelry besides some simple earrings and a necklace. Rings always felt odd on my fingers when I tried them on. This one, Jeff's engagement ring, felt as if I'd always worn it.

I was still naked, sitting on the bed, chilled by the morning air, Jeff's free hand skimming up my ribs. The damp towel around his waist was tucked in near one hip, coming loose as he sat next to me. I kissed him, reached for the edge of his towel and worked it loose, pulled it free so he was bare to me. I trailed my fingers up his thigh to his sack, massaged it in my fingers.

Jeff growled, twisted on the bed, and in the space of a single heartbeat had me flat on my back, his cock probing my entrance and sliding in.

"You just showered," I said, caressing the ridged muscles of his broad, powerful back.

"I'll shower again," he said, tangling the fingers of both our hands together above our heads. "Say it again, Anna. I heard you, but I'm not sure it's sunk in yet."

I smiled, wrapping my legs around his ass and pulling him deeper into me. "I want to marry you, Jeff." I rolled my hips, feeling him slide deep and slip out. "Has it sunk in yet?"

He laughed, moving into me in a serpentine glide. "I don't know. I might need to hear it once more."

"I love you, Jeff..." My breath was ragged, my motions desperate as Jeff brought me to climax almost instantly. "I'll marry you."

He buried his face in my neck as he came with me. "Oh, god, Anna...you don't know what it means to me...oh, god...hearing you say that."

"I don't know why I hesitated," I said, as we moved together. "We belong together."

"We always have," Jeff whispered. "It just took you longer to see it."

"I see it now."

I did see it. Sweat mingling, breath merging, pleasure synchronizing the beating of our hearts, I knew then I would only ever love him, be with him. I couldn't fathom, in that moment, how I'd ever missed it.

In moments of sharing love so powerful it winds the fabric of your soul around his, you can't help but feel the perfection of true intimacy. It goes beyond the sharing of physical sensation, it goes deeper than the vulnerability of nakedness, or the expression of emotional connection. It becomes an instant of timeless unity, in which you and he cease to be discrete identities and become something new, something more.

You become each other for those brief eternities spent clinging together in sweat-slick surrender.

When compared to such raw completion, marriage ceases to be quite so frightening, and begins to seem the most natural next step: binding yourself, your whole self, voluntarily, to the man who knows you most deeply.

Chapter 2

I TWISTED JEFF'S RING around my finger nervously. A cup of coffee sat untouched in front of me, tendrils of steam rising from the tawny liquid. My heart thrummed, my stomach flopped, and my mind raced.

What the hell am I going to say?

My purse sat open on the booth bench next to me. The black box containing Chase's ring stared at me, daring me to think I could do this without completely losing it.

"You sure you don't want nothin' to eat, hon?" the waitress asked.

I shook my head and willed her to leave me alone. I needed these minutes before Chase showed up to get my nerves under control. The last thing I could do right then was eat. Which should say a lot about how nervous I was. Food was normally my greatest comfort. A piece of pie, or an order of fries with ranch, or a bowl of chicken lemon rice soup would usually soothe me under most any circumstances.

These weren't usual circumstances.

I'd never broken anyone's heart before.

I saw his black Ducati pull into a parking spot, and I nearly vomited just watching him stride into the Denny's where we'd agreed to meet. It was public, which was bittersweet. I knew I needed a buffer against him. I didn't want to do this in public, but I didn't think I could handle being near him in private. I knew myself better than that.

He slid into the bench across from me, unzipping his leather jacket. He ran his palm over the sandpaper stubble on his scalp, heaved a deep breath, and planted his elbows on the table.

"This isn't a good news meeting, is it?" he asked.

I shook my head, not trusting my voice yet. I sipped my coffee, burning my tongue.

"Well, then, out with it," he said. "Don't beat around the bush."

My breath trembled as I drew it in to speak. "Ican'tmarryyou."

Chase laughed. "Slow it down. I'm not gonna faint, okay? When you wanted to meet me here, at a fucking Denny's, I knew what the answer was going to be."

"I'm sorry, Chase. I just—I can't be around you in private. It's too hard." I sipped my coffee again, more to buy time to think than anything else. "I care about you. I had a really great time with you, and I can't thank you enough for what you've done for me, but—"

"But I'm not enough. Not good enough."

"Goddamn it, Chase. No. You are amazing. You're an incredible lover, a great guy, and—"

"If you say, 'you'll make some woman really happy someday, but it's just not me,' I swear to god I'll lose my fucking mind," Chase said.

He flagged down a waitress and ordered a cup of coffee.

"I don't know what else to say. It's the truth. You're amazing, and you deserve someone amazing. I'm not that someone. It's cliché and stupid and I hate the way that sounds, like it's a line from a bad romance movie. But it's true."

The waitress brought Chase's coffee, giving him a long, hungry once-over before walking away; Chase seemed oblivious to her attention.

Chase stared into his coffee. "It's not just about me, is it." It was phrased like a question, but his tone made it a statement.

"What do you mean?"

"I mean, is it that you don't love me, or that you love *him* more?"

I hesitated for a long moment before answering. "A little of both, I guess. I love Jeff, with all my heart. He...he asked me to marry him the day before you—before you showed up. I would have said yes anyway. You coming here like you did, it really threw me off. I do care about you, Chase. Maybe, yeah, there might be a part of me that wonders if I could have fallen in love with you. If we could have been great together. But...all the rest of me says I belong with Jeff."

He dumped several creamers into his coffee and followed it with several packets of sugar, stirring it until it sloshed over the side and ran down to pool on the table. He drank his coffee too fast, staring over the top into the middle distance.

"I should have come after you sooner," he muttered, almost to himself rather than me.

"I don't think it would have mattered, Chase. Maybe if you had followed me to Detroit that same day, and forced me to listen to you then, *maybe*. But do we really want to play 'what if'? I don't. It is what it is."

Chase growled. "I hate that phrase. It's so empty and...fucking meaningless. 'It is what it is.' Just another way of saying, 'I don't feel like coming up with a real explanation.'"

"Haven't I given you an explanation?" I asked, irritation replacing nerves. "I told you honestly what I'm feeling, and why I'm saying no."

"I still think you could have loved me, if you had given it a chance. But you didn't, and now it's too late." Chase's voice was low and thick with emotion.

"I don't know what to tell you. What if part of the reason I ran like I did was because I knew it wouldn't have worked? I don't want to end up like my parents. They had a great physical relationship, but nothing else. I think that's us."

Chase's gaze snapped to mine, and he slammed his mug down. "You think that's all we have? That's all I'm good for?"

"God, Chase, quit being so damn melodramatic. No, that's not what I think. You're good for more than sex. I think you're sweet and talented and so much else. But I do wonder. Is that all we have? I don't know. Maybe not. But the question is there, and that's reason enough for me."

"And you know you have more with Jeff."

"This isn't about Jeff. I'm not talking to you about Jeff."

"Do you talk to him about me? About us?"

He's not taking this well. I didn't know how he would take it, but I wasn't expecting this.

"Chase, that's not the point." I focused on breathing and sipping coffee until I was calm enough to be rational. "What else do you want me to say? Do you need to hear it bluntly? I do not want to be with you. I want to be with Jeff."

Chase took a deep, shuddering breath. He wouldn't meet my eyes. "I guess that's it then. Hearing you say it that way..."

I placed the ring box on the table in front of him, next to his coffee. Chase gingerly opened the lid, took another shudder-wracked breath. He was barely keeping it together, I realized. My own eyes burned, feeling the hurt radiating off him.

He lifted the ring out of the box, stared at it for a second, then put it back. He slapped the lid closed and put the box in an inside pocket of his leather jacket. He finished his coffee, silence aching between us.

"Bye, Anna. Good luck with life."

He slid out of the booth and practically ran out of the Denny's. As he turned away, I could have sworn I saw him touch his eye, like a tear was streaking his face, but then he was gone, leaving me to wonder. His bike roared to life, and he peeled out of the parking lot at a breakneck pace.

I managed to keep it together long enough to pay the bill for both coffees and get into my car before I broke down. I cried long and hard for Chase. He had given me something priceless in my newfound confidence, my belief in my own beauty and sexual power. I didn't think he could ever understand that, and I wished I'd tried to impart some of that to him, but it was too late.

I forced myself to stop crying. I'd cried more in the last few days than I had in most of the rest of my life. It was done, he was gone, and I could move on. I could go back to being happy with Jeff.

I drove home, found a note from Jeff on my counter:

Anna,

Had to go help an old Army buddy move. I'll be back later this evening and we'll go out. I've got reservations at Maggiano's.

If you need to talk, call me. Hope things went well. You know what I mean. I love you.

Jeff. XOXO

Yes, he actually wrote "X"s and "O"s on the bottom of the note. It was cute enough to make my heart melt even further. I folded the note and put it in my purse, along with all the other notes Jeff had written me. I wasn't sure why I was saving them, other than it felt wrong to throw them away.

My roommate Jamie came home not long after I did. We'd rarely seen each other lately, as we were both gone a lot. She always had a boyfriend, someone to spend the time with, but it was never serious. I'd spent most of my time at Jeff's lately, so this was the first time I'd seen her since our conversation after I got back from New York.

"Anna, I feel like I haven't seen you in forever," Jamie said, giving me a hug.

I hugged her back, holding tight. "It's been a while," I agreed.

"You've been with Jeff, then?" she asked, pulling away and looking at me.

Being my best friend, she sees everything in my eyes. But she still asks.

"Tell me."

"There's nothing to tell," I said. Talking about it would only upset me all over again.

"Bullshit," Jamie said.

She dumped her purse on the table, stuck the charger in her phone, and plopped down at the kitchen table, sipping from her venti skinny white chocolate mocha. She always got the same thing from Starbucks. I teased her about it pretty relentlessly, since she's never, ever had anything else for as long as she's been going to Starbucks.

"It's not bullshit. I don't want to talk about it."

"So there is something." Jamie rolled her eyes and sighed. "You know you're going to tell me. It just depends on how much wine I have to ply you with first."

"Ugh. You are such a pain in the ass," I said.

"Yep. That's why I'm your best friend. We pry information from each other when necessary. This is one of those times. I can see it in your eyes. You've been crying."

"All right. Fine. Let me make some tea first."
I filled the carafe from the refrigerator, set it on
the warmer, and depressed the button. When the
water had heated, I poured it over two bags of Irish
Breakfast tea, added sugar, and sat down next to
Jamie.

"All hell broke loose, Jay," I said, by way of
introduction.

"Uh-oh."

"Yeah. Jeff forgave me. We got back together,
and things were great. *Are* great. Now, at least.
But...he proposed." I showed her my hand, with
his ring on my finger.

Jamie spewed coffee into her hand. "What?"
She wiped at her face and hands with a napkin.
"He *what*?" She took my hand in hers, practically
yanking me over the table to examine the ring.

I withdrew my hand after a minute, staring at
the ring myself. "He proposed. Asked me to marry
him."

Jamie shrieked, clapping. "Tell me! Spill!
Now!"

I laughed. "Jesus, Jay! Calm down! I'm spilling,
already. He took me on a picnic—"

"Like, an actual, factual picnic? Like, outside?
With a blanket and a basket of food—?"

"Yes, Jay," I cut in. "An actual, factual picnic.
Beneath a huge oak tree, on a handmade quilt, with
a basket of food and champagne and everything. It

was…so romantic. We had this *incredible* sex, and afterward, he pulled one of those little black boxes from his pants pocket and proposed."

"And you said yes, right?" I didn't answer immediately, and Jamie freaked. "Oh. My. God. You didn't. You *hesitated*."

"I was scared! You know how I am about marriage, and my parents. I…yeah. I hesitated. I told him I needed to think about it."

"You needed to think about it." Jamie repeated my words like they were an accusation. "You're an idiot. If he loves you, and you love him, what is there to think about?"

"I'm not done, Jay," I sipped my steaming tea, and then started again. "He took it pretty well, I guess. Told me he understood how it might be a surprise and to take as much time as I needed. I wanted to say yes, I really did, but I just…I couldn't. Some part of me wouldn't let me. I don't know. Well, we had a gig the next day. At the fucking Dive, of all places."

"Isn't that where you used to sing with Chase?"

I nodded. "Yeah. Exactly. Well, we get through the shift okay, and then I took a break near the end. When I came back in, Jeff had this weird look on his face. I wasn't sure what to make of it, but then I saw *him*."

"No! Chase showed up?" Jamie covered her mouth with a hand, leaning forward.

"Just wait. It gets better."

"How could it get better?" Jamie demanded. "Jeff proposes, you say 'I'll think about it,' and then Chase shows up?"

"He looked different, so I didn't recognize him at first. He'd shaved his head—"

"Oooh! Does it look good on him? Not all guys can pull off that look."

"Yes, of course it looks good on him. The man can make a paper bag look sexy. With his head shaved, his eyes are just that much more vivid. He'd also gauged his ears and gotten a new tatt, and I'm not always a huge fan of ear gauging, but again, it's Chase, so it works."

"What happened?" Jamie slapped the table. "Get on with it!"

"You're the one who keeps interrupting!" I said, exasperated. "So *any*way, I saw him, but I didn't have time to do anything. He has a microphone, and he's got the lights on him, and he turns, sees me coming in from the side door, and he fixes me with this intense, typical Chase stare. Now, keep in mind I haven't seen or spoken to him since New York. He called and left all these voicemails, sent me a million texts. You remember. Well, I didn't answer any of them. It had been over a month since I'd been back here, and it had seemed like he'd given up. So then he shows up out of the blue, where I'm working. With Jeff, who just proposed.

Of course, Chase had no way of knowing that, but still."

"What did he do? What'd he say?"

"God, impatient much? I'm getting there. So he's got everyone's attention. He just...he commands the room, you know? He doesn't even have to try. He's got that larger-than-life magnetism. So everyone was looking. I mean everyone.

"And then he proposed."

"*What?* Are you fucking serious?" Jamie seemed nearly apoplectic. "He shows up out of the blue, after not having spoken to you in, like, two months, and then he asks you to marry him? In public?"

"Exactly. I nearly had a heart attack. I mean for real, I think my heart actually did skip a few beats."

"What did you do?"

"I freaked! I ran like a bat out of hell. I swear, in the seconds before I ran out the door, you could hear a pin drop. I've heard the expression before, you know? But have you ever actually been in a room full of people that is completely and totally silent, with every single eye on you, waiting for your response? It's absolutely terrifying. It's worse than fucking up a performance. With that, you have the music to prompt you, you can keep going and everyone knows, but the song keeps going. This was so much worse. I wanted to die."

Jamie, for all her bravado and manic energy, truly did love me and understand me. "Oh, honey. I can't even begin to imagine what that must have been like. How did Jeff take it?"

I winced. "He had a glass of Coke in his hand when Chase proposed, and he actually squeezed the glass so hard it shattered. Naturally enough, his first thought must have been that I'd been talking to Chase behind his back or something. But I think when he saw my reaction he knew I hadn't been. Chase and Jeff both ran after me, and...Jeff tried to push Chase away, saying something like, 'you've had your turn'—"

"Oh, god, that couldn't have gone well."

"No, not even a little bit. Chase pushed him back, and Jeff decked him. I mean, he leveled him. Completely flattened him. And let me tell you, having two guys fight over you is not in any way cool. It's awful. I mean, having your guy protect you from some asshole is one thing. I can see how that'd be hot. But when you care about both of them? It's heartbreaking."

"God, Anna. How awful."

"Yeah. So I made Jeff go inside and told Chase I couldn't deal with him right then. I don't think Chase understood at first how I might not have completely appreciated a proposal quite like that."

"Idiot."

"No, he meant well. He just wanted to get my attention, I guess. I'd run off and ignored him, and he was upset. I don't say it was the best way of doing it, but I can understand where he's coming from." I sighed before making the next admission. "You were right about Chase, and my feelings for him, and all that, though. He'd—"

"Well, of course I was," Jamie said, waving her hand as if it was the most obvious thing in the world. "I knew it, I just knew it would take you time to realize it yourself."

She peered at me, and then the ring. "Wait, so is that Jeff's ring or Chase's? I thought it was Jeff, but if you're admitting you have feelings for Chase, then I'm not so sure, all of a sudden."

"I do have feelings for Chase. But what I realized was they were more like my mom and dad's feelings for each other. I wasn't sure we had an emotional relationship. He's great, honestly. It's not that I don't think he's capable of having that kind of relationship, 'cause I think he totally is. I just don't think it's there for him and I. Him and me, he and I—whatever."

"I think it'd be 'him and me.'"

"Oh, like you have any idea," I teased. "But seriously, though. Chase is amazing, in a lot of ways. But I don't think we have a relationship that would last forever. The sex would stop being exciting, or...well, no, it wouldn't. But a relationship has to have more than sex to it, or it doesn't work. I learned that from my parents."

Jamie was conspicuously silent, staring through the tiny hole in the lid of her cup at the dregs of her mocha.

"You'll find him, Jay," I said, quietly, laying my hand over hers. "Just stop looking for a while. Just be content being you. Go without sex for a few months. When you find the right guy, it'll be that much more amazing."

"A few *months*? I can't go a few *days*, Anna. I'd die. I'd be a cranky bitch." She curled her lip in disgust. "God, what does that say about me? Am I a nympho? I am, aren't I? I'm an actual nymphomaniac A sex addict."

"You are not. You're just trying to fill the hole in your heart with sex, like I do with food. It won't work, though. That's what I'm learning."

"Why are we talking about me?" Jamie said. "Shut up about me. I'll be fine. So what did you do?"

"I met Chase for lunch the next day and told him I'd give him a chance to explain, but that it wouldn't change anything. So he went and tried to get me to marry him anyway. He was charming and convincing and totally Chase. And it was confusing as hell. He gave me a ring, and he told me to think about it. I went home and cried my eyes out, and then Jeff showed up."

"What did he do?"

"He…he reminded me why I'm so completely in love with him. He didn't push me on his proposal at all. He didn't even bring it up. He knew I was upset, and he comforted me. He let me talk about what was bugging me, and he actually listened, even though it was about him and Chase. He…he's so much more than I can ever deserve. He always thinks about me first. He told me he loved me enough to let me go, if I decided I wanted to be with Chase instead. He just wanted me to be happy."

"He said that?" Jamie seemed choked up at the idea, though she kept it under control.

"Yeah. He just held me, let me talk, let me cry. When a guy knows whether to just hold you and let you cry or talk to you and try to make it better, you know he really knows your heart."

"And Jeff knows you like that?"

"Yes, he does."

"So is that when you knew?"

I shook my head. "No. I knew when I couldn't imagine a day without him in it. I knew when making love to him wasn't just a physical thing anymore. It was an all of me thing."

Jamie slipped the cardboard sleeve off the paper cup and started ripping it into pieces, not looking at me. "Sounds great."

"Jamie—"

"No, seriously. I'm happy for you. Jealous as hell, I don't mind admitting." She finally met my eyes. "If you fuck this up with Jeff, I swear I will kill you."

"I know. Believe me, I know."

"So you said yes to Jeff?"

"Yeah. Last night. I saw Chase today. I got back from talking to him just before you did."

"So you told Chase no, then?" Jamie asked. I nodded. "How did he take it?"

"Not well. Not well at all. I mean, how do you take something like that? Is there a good way?" I ripped the tag from the tea bag between my fingers and added it to the pile Jamie was making with the cup sleeve. "He argued. He protested. He was mad."

"Can you blame him? You're amazing. And you didn't really give him a chance, did you?"

I shrugged. "It doesn't matter. I'm convinced it wouldn't have worked. I love Jeff. I belong with Jeff."

"So did Chase go back to New York?"

"I don't know. I'm assuming so."

Silence for a bit, then, "So when is the wedding?"

I laughed. "I don't know. We haven't exactly discussed any of that yet. I just told him yes last night, and I haven't seen him yet today. He's helping a buddy move. We're going out later."

Jamie nodded and stood up, scooped our trash into her empty cup, and threw it away. "Well, like I

said, I'm glad for you. I'll help you plan your wedding when you're ready. Just…be smart, okay? I
love you too much to watch you mess this up."

"What's that mean?" I asked, irritated. "Why
do you keep thinking I'd mess this up?"

She shrugged. "Because we're alike. And I'd
totally mess it up."

"Give yourself more credit, Jay. And me."

She laughed as she closed her bedroom door.
"Credit where credit is due, Anna. You nearly did
mess it up, you know." She opened the door again,
poked her head out, and said, "If Chase shows up
again, just say no. And then send him my way."

I just sighed at that. She was incorrigible.

I took a shower and spent a long time doing my
hair and makeup for my date with Jeff later that
night. I was still wrapped in a towel, not having
decided on what to wear, when the door buzzed.
I was expecting Jeff, so I didn't even think twice
about hitting the buzzer and opening my apartment door. My towel was loosely wrapped around
my chest, a toothbrush in my mouth as I held the
door open. Expecting Jeff, I started to loosen the
towel, thinking I would give him a surprise before
we left. The thought had my juices flowing, anticipation of Jeff's hands on me, his lips on me.

Chase clumped in his shit-kicker boots into the
entryway. Shock hit me like a bolt of lightning. I
started to close the door in his face, simply out of

self-preservation. His eyes were dark with desire, his hands shoved into the pockets of his tight leather pants, stubble smeared across his face and scalp. His face was twisted with a haze of emotion, and I felt the familiar rush of uncontrollable desire for him pierce through me, riding the heat of my already aroused hormones.

He took a step toward me, and then another. I backed up one step, but then he caught me in his strong arms and crushed me against him.

Conflict warred in me. I struggled with my desire, with guilt, struggled against his implacable strength.

And then he kissed me, and I was lost.

Chapter 3

MY HEAD SWIRLED, whirled, skirled. Lunacy and madness boiled in my brain, heat moved within me in convection circles of desire, clouding my heart and body.

I pushed against him, or I thought I did. I intended to, meant to. But somehow I was moving into the living room, the back of my thighs bumping against the edge of the couch. I moaned, meaning to say "no," but all that emerged from between our locked lips was the moan. It sounded, even to me, all too much like encouragement. My body was betraying my heart and mind. I knew this was wrong. I didn't even *want* this. Not really. I didn't love Chase.

But his lips burned against mine, his tongue explored my mouth, my gums and teeth and tongue. His hands were branding my arms, sliding down to the damp towel, touching the swell of my hips and then up the silk of my thighs.

No, no, not this, not like this. My thoughts were fragments of denial.

I lifted my hands to his chest and pushed, pushed, *pushed*. He didn't budge. He only kissed me harder. His fingers brushed the dip of my hip where leg met pubic bone. So close, and I knew all too well how much fire he could spread in my body with a single finger.

No! The word wouldn't come out.

His hand slipped up my front, spreading the edges of the towel apart to reveal my skin, my belly, my breasts, and then the wet terrycloth was falling down around me and I was bare to the air, my breasts crushed against the cotton of his black T-shirt, my pussy brushing against the supple leather of his pants, his erection hard against my belly.

Fingers brushed the bottom of one breast, traced a circle around my nipple, traitorously erect. I forced my body to remain still, to not arch into his touch.

I heard footsteps on the stairs. The front door was wide open. Anyone walking by could see me, naked, clutched to Chase, lips locked in a kiss.

If Jeff sees me like this, he'll never forgive me.

The thought provided enough impetus to rip away from Chase. I pushed with all my strength against him, stumbled backward, tripping over my towel.

"No!" The word scraped past my throat, a ragged denial. "No, Chase! I'm not with you. I can't do this. I don't want to do this. Go. Just…go."

I crouched, one arm across my breasts, the other across my privates, to lift my towel and wrap it awkwardly around me. Chase had seen me naked, making a mockery of my modesty, but to me it was a gesture of refusal.

"Anna, please, I know you said we weren't right for each other, but I couldn't just leave, not without—"

"Barging into my home and jumping me?" I was angry, now, embarrassed. I couldn't see past Chase's broad shoulders, but I felt a presence beyond him. "The door is wide open, Chase. Do you even *care* what I want?"

"But we've been together before, in other places—"

"That's *over*, Chase. *We* are over." Anger was quickly ebbing away, stealing my strength. "You need to leave. Please. Just leave."

Chase didn't move. He just stood there staring at me, eyes wavering, alternating between the hard anger of rejection and the soft hurt of love denied. He took a step toward me, and I backed away.

I heard Jamie's door open behind me, but I didn't turn to look at her. I heard a foot shuffle on the carpet behind Chase. I squeezed my eyes closed in a vain, wishing for none of this to have happened. I could feel Jeff's anger, even without seeing him. It was a palpable force.

I stepped to the side, and there was Jeff, dressed in pressed khakis and a crisp white button-down, sleeves rolled up to just beneath the elbow. His brown hair was getting longer, enough to run my fingers through, and his dark brown eyes were blazing.

"Jeff, it's not what you—"

"Shut up, Anna," he said, his voice calm and deadly quiet. He turned his eyes to Chase. "I'll give you one chance to walk the fuck away before I break you in half, pretty boy."

Chase seemed to swell up, get bigger. His fists clenched. I knew what was coming, and I had to stop it.

"No!" I stepped forward, pushing Chase between the shoulder blades. "Just go, Chase! Get the fuck out! Go! I don't want you here!"

Chase turned to me. "Anna, I'm sorry, I just—"

The anger in Jeff's eyes, directed at me, it seemed, spurred me to scream, "*GO!*"

Chase's face closed down, turned hard and impenetrable. He spun on his heel and stalked past Jeff, who closed his eyes, fists trembling, jaw clenched, as if it was taking all his restraint to keep his hands to himself.

Chase paused with one foot on the stair, then turned back. "This was all me, Jeff," he said. "This wasn't her. Don't be mad at her." Then he was gone.

Jeff's eyes flicked to me, taking in the towel clutched to my breasts, hanging down my front so my bare hips peeked out from the sides of the towel.

I heard Jamie's soft footfalls behind me, then she was in front of me, as if to shield me. I backed up, bumped against the wall and slid down to my bottom, letting the towel pool over my lap.

"Jeff, he just showed up, okay?" Jamie said. "He took her by surprise. Don't—"

"Give us a minute, Jamie, will you?"

"Jeff—"

"It'll be fine. I'm fine. She's fine. We're fine. Just...go make sure he's gone, okay?"

Jamie searched Jeff's face, seemed to see something that satisfied her, and left, closing the door behind her.

Jeff turned to me, and suddenly his face was soft once more, the anger gone. He crouched in front of me, lifted the towel to cover me. He took my hands and lifted me to my feet. Adrenaline had been rushing through me, but it abandoned me right then, and my knees buckled. Jeff caught me, lifted me effortlessly, carried me into my room, closed the door behind us with his heel, and set me on the bed.

The bed dipped as he sat beside me, brushing my hair out of my face. "Everything is okay, Anna," he said. "I saw what happened."

"What'd you see?" I could barely muster a whisper.

"I came up the stairs and saw your door standing open. I panicked for a second. I worried someone had broken in, but then I saw pretty—I saw Chase kissing you. I saw red, and I nearly lost it. I wanted to rip him apart."

"He just showed up," I said. "I thought it was you coming up. I had just gotten out of the shower, so I was in my towel. I was...I was thinking we could...you know, before we went to dinner so I was...turned on. I was thinking about you. I wanted you. And then it was him, and he didn't even say anything. He just walked in the open door and kissed me. I didn't want him to kiss me, I swear. It took me by so much surprise that I couldn't think. And...I honestly do have this automatic reaction to him. I know you'll probably think it's bullshit, but it's like this instinctive reaction, and I can't control it. I just...can't think."

Jeff's mouth opened, but I spoke over him.

"I tried to stop it right away, but I couldn't—"

"Did he force you?" Jeff asked. The anger in his eyes flared up again.

"No, not like that. No. He didn't hurt me, and he would have stopped. He did stop, when I managed to get myself together and tell him to. I don't know why—I can't—"

"I get it, Anna." He took my hands in his, tugged me toward him. "I saw. You pushed him away. I heard what you said."

"You're not mad at me?" I was suddenly shaking, terrified, even though he was still here holding my hands, that he'd leave me. "I heard your footsteps on the stairs, and I—I knew if you saw him kissing me, you'd—you'd leave, you wouldn't love me."

Jeff pulled me to my feet and pressed our bodies together, holding the sheet in place. "I love you. I admit, when I first saw you guys like you were, I did think you'd chosen him after all. I was set to walk away."

"Jeff, I don't know what it is with him. I know I'm not in love with him. And I didn't want him to kiss me. But when he did, I still felt...I don't know how to put it—"

Jeff cut me off. "Anna, you had a thing with him. He's a good-looking guy. I can see how he'd be exciting to be around, I really do. Don't like to think about you with him, but I can see it."

"That's it exactly. He was exciting. He *is* exciting." I wrapped my arms around his waist. "But he's not you."

"And I'm not exciting," Jeff said with a lift of his eyebrow.

"Jeff, you're exactly who you're supposed to be, and that's who I'm in love with. Exciting wears off. For me, at least. You're what I want."

"So you like me even though I'm boring, huh?" Jeff smiled as he said it to make it seem like a joke, but I sensed he wasn't entirely kidding.

"You're not boring," I said. "You're exciting in your own way."

"How's that?"

"You're sexy. You're sweet and steady and considerate. You're amazing in bed."

"Steady?" Another inquisitive lift of the eyebrow.

"Yeah, steady. Dependable. Responsible." I planted a kiss on his jaw next to his chin.

His mouth slanted down to catch mine. "Those aren't exciting traits, sweetheart."

"No, but they're yours, and they're what I've fallen in love with. You're always there when I need you. I don't think a lot of guys would have stuck around long enough to find out the truth about what just happened. They would've taken one look and run." I ran my fingertips through his hair, tracing around his ear to the back of his head. "You didn't. You gave me the benefit of the doubt."

"Yeah, that part wasn't easy. I knew you liked him, and I had to wonder if maybe you liked him more, since he was all rock star and whatever. Leather pants and tattoos and shit."

"You could wear leather pants," I said, smiling at the mental image.

"I'd look stupid," Jeff said.

"I don't know about that," I said. "I think you might look pretty damn sexy."

"Hmmm. Don't know about that."

"Maybe I'll buy you a pair. You can wear them just for me."

"Guess we'll see." Jeff's palms ran over my shoulders and smoothed down my spine, stopping at the swell of my ass. "You should get dressed, or we won't make it to dinner."

His eyes were wide and dark with desire, now. I wanted to erase the memory of the last ten minutes from my mind, and his. I leaned away from him to let the towel drop to the floor between us. Jeff breathed deeply, his nostrils flaring, his eyes raking down my body.

"We have a few minutes, don't we?" I breathed.

"Maybe just a few," Jeff agreed, pushing me backward to my room.

I let him push me until the door was closed behind us, then, keeping my eyes locked on his, I turned to face the bed, climbed up on to it on all fours and presented my ass to him.

Jeff grinned, reaching for his belt buckle. I watched him over my shoulder as he stripped down. He was about to take his socks off when I spoke up.

"Leave the socks on," I suggested.

He paused. "Why? Isn't that weird? Sex in socks?"

I giggled. "Sex in socks. Sounds like a kinky Dr. Seuss book. It's funny. A guy wearing nothing but a giant hard on and dress socks is just...funny, in a hot sort of way."

Jeff laughed crawling onto the bed behind me. "Sex in socks it is, then." He knelt behind me, running his hands over my ass, up my back and down again. "You look so hot like this, all spread out for me."

"Come on, Jeff, take the leap, put it in and take me deep," I said, in a sing-songy Dr. Seuss voice.

Jeff sputtered into laughter, bending over me. "Oh, god, Anna. You did *not* just rhyme at me, did you?"

"I think I did. Can you come up with anything better, kid?"

Jeff slid his palm up the inside of my thighs, a slow and gentle touch. His finger drifted up to my spread opening, dipped in and back out. "Of course I can rhyme. I'm a singer, I do it all the time."

He spoke in a soft lilting voice, slipping two fingers into me, curling into my G-spot and scraping across it. His other hand joined his first, brushing across my clit with his finger, drawing a gasp from me.

"That doesn't count—we're rhyming about sex. I wanna see those muscles flex."

"When it comes to rhyming, you kind of suck." He touched drew his finger around my clit in slow circles until my hips began to rock with his rhythm.

"Quit talking so…we can fuck," I gasped.

Jeff laughed, a deep rumble in his chest as he delved his two fingers deeper into my wet pussy, then pulled out and touched his pinky finger to my other, tighter hole. I sucked in a sharp breath at the unexpected contact, then relaxed and pushed back into his hand, encouraging him. He pressed lightly at first, pulsing with his pinky in slow waves until I felt the hard ring of muscles give way, allowing his smallest finger in. My entire body convulsed as he pushed in, ever so carefully. Each time he circled my clit, causing me to quiver and buck my hips, he pushed a little deeper with his pinky.

I collapsed forward onto my forearms, my face buried in the blanket as he penetrated me, unable to think or string words together. My thighs shook with the onset of orgasm, and as the climax rose, I felt Jeff remove his fingers from my pussy and replace them with the broad tip of his cock, touching at first, splitting my nether lips with his hot, hard head.

His pinky stayed in place, though, and when he thrust himself slowly in, he matched his inward pulse with his pinky. My hands fisted into the covers and I pulled myself forward as he pulled out, then, with a shuddering outbreath, slammed my body backward into him.

I couldn't stop the muffled shriek from escaping my lips as his finger drove into me to the last knuckle, his cock driving into my farthest wall. Jeff growled low in his throat, one hand gripping my hip and pulling me into him. He was holding himself to his typical Jeff pace, slow and deep strokes. I wanted him to lose control, if only for a moment. I rocked my hips again, a high-pitched gasp erupting from me, and I felt Jeff jerk into me, once, hard, and then force himself to slow down and go gently.

I turned my head to look at him over my shoulder. His eyes were closed, his head thrown back, his spine arched into a curve as he pushed into me. I rolled my hips, a small pulse at first, and his lips parted as he matched the thrust; I moved harder, and he thrust in synch with me.

I began to rock my ass onto his cock with desperate force, feeling the orgasm still bubbling inside me, not quite there yet, but so close. I let my need overtake me, still watching Jeff as he began to sway forward, bending at the waist to crash harder and harder. His palm slid up my back to rest between my shoulder blades, and I rose up on my hands again, shuddering back and forth with my entire body to meet his thrusts.

Now the climax rose again, and this time it boiled through me, cresting as he came inside me, growling through gritted teeth as he thrust hard, fast, and relentless. I let my voice rise unfettered to match his, plunging backward into his crushing thrusts, wave after wave of orgasm blinding me, ripping screams from me, pleasure so potent it seemed nearly painful threading between the pulses of my heartbeat, the pulses of Jeff's hard body against my soft one.

The waves lessened with the slowing of his thrusts, leaving me limp on the bed. Jeff extracted himself from me and lay down beside me.

"God, every time I think making love to you can't get more intense…" Jeff said, panting.

"I swear it gets better every time," I said, "which I didn't think was possible."

Jeff curled up behind me, kissing the back of my neck. "I can't believe you started rhyming."

"It was pretty cheesy, wasn't it?"

He laughed, his breath huffing hot on my skin. "It was awful. But cute."

"Awful?" I protested, twisting in his arms to face him. "Like your rhymes were any better?"

He just laughed and kissed me. "Of course they were. Let's go get cleaned up again."

We rinsed off, dressed, and left, barely making our reservation in time. Jeff seemed distracted through dinner. I let it go until the very end of our meal.

I sipped from my wine and then reached for Jeff's hand. "What's bugging you?" I asked.

"Nothing's bugging me," he said, idly twisting the ring on my finger.

"Okay, whatever," I said, my voice dripping with sarcasm.

He grunted a laugh. "Fine, then. I guess I'm just wondering, now that you've agreed to marry me, how long of an engagement you're thinking."

"I hadn't really thought about it at all, honestly. I've only had, like, a day to get used to the idea that I said yes." I rolled the cloth napkin into a tight spiral. "What are you thinking?"

He shrugged. "I don't know, either. I know I love you, and I'm personally ready whenever you are. If it were only up to me, I'd say only as long as it took to plan the wedding."

"The wedding," I said.

Agreeing to marry him had seemed simple and natural enough, but I hadn't given a thought to the actual wedding yet. I'd been pretty preoccupied with other concerns, after all.

"Yeah, the wedding. I thought all girls spent their time planning the whole thing out with their girlfriends?"

I laughed. "Well, yeah, but by the time you're an adult, things have changed, you know? Like I said the other night, I never saw myself getting married. I don't know. I haven't really thought about it much. I guess I'm not a typical girl like that."

Jeff smiled. "Baby, there's nothing typical about you, and that's exactly what I love about you. This just means we can figure it out together."

"I thought guys hated planning weddings. Just agree to whatever his fiancée wants, and all that."

"Well, I'm no more a typical guy than you are a typical girl. I want to be a part of it."

"I guess not. So we're a matched pair like that, huh?"

"Guess we are. So where do you start planning one of these things, anyway? I don't have any idea."

"Neither do I, really," I admitted, "but I'd say location? Or date?"

"Hmmm. Do we want it around here? Like in a church?"

I laughed. "Where else would you have a wedding but in a church?"

Jeff frowned at me. "Um, outside? On a beach?"

"Oh, good point. So what do you want?"

"I don't know. I like the idea of something fun. On a beach in Florida, maybe? Or even somewhere more exotic, like Jamaica?"

"You know how expensive that would be?"

He shrugged. "Yeah, suppose it would be kinda pricey, but worth it, to my thinking."

I tried to picture myself on a beach, somewhere tropical, in a wedding dress, facing Jeff. "It would be awesome, wouldn't it? And it's not like there'd be a lot of people to invite."

That sobered Jeff up quickly. "Guess not. For either of us, huh? I'd invite my mom and brother, probably Darren, my buddy from the Army."

Who would I invite to my wedding?

"There really isn't anyone for me besides Jamie," I said, the realization hurting more than I'd anticipated.

"Oh, come on," Jeff said. "I know you don't have the best relationship with your mom, but you'd at least invite her to your wedding, wouldn't you?"

I shrugged, uncomfortable with the direction of the conversation. "I don't know. I haven't seen her in a long time. Years."

Jeff's brow furrowed. "Really? Not even for holidays?"

I stared into the rippling red surface of my wine. "Jamie and I both are pretty much alone, so we've spent the last few holidays together. Her past is even more messed up than mine, if you'll believe it."

"Except for the other morning, I've never really heard you talk about your parents much. Or your past at all, come to think of it." He frowned into his wine glass. "Actually, I don't even know if you have any siblings. I've known you for six years. How is it I don't know that?"

"I don't talk about it. Nothing to say." I shrugged, trying for a casual dismissal.

Jeff didn't buy it. "Come on, Anna. Talk to me."

I set my glass down. "There's not much to say. I have an older brother in the Marines, career. Joined up the day he graduated high school, eight years ago now. Then there's my cousin who lives in Miami. She's got her own life. We used to be close, except for every other weekend. But she got married as soon as she could and moved to Miami."

"You don't talk to her, either?"

I shrugged again. "We email back and forth a few times a month. I went down to visit her and her family...I think it was last summer? When I went to Florida a while ago."

"Last summer. I remember you going to Florida," Jeff said. "So you'd invite her at least, right?"

"Yeah, I suppose I would. Miri is great. She and her husband Kyle have boys, twins."

"Twins? Does that run in your family? Or is it from her husband's side?"

"You're really full of twenty questions tonight, aren't you?" I asked.

"I want to know you. I realized after talking about your folks how little I know about your family."

"Family." I spat the word, said it like a swear word. "I don't like my parents. That sounds awful, I guess, but it's the truth. There's a reason I don't talk to them. Or about them. My dad...he was the problem. Hopeless drunk. Held a job no problem, but he'd drink a bottle of Jack like it was nothing. Smacked us around a bit. Mom, mainly, me and Jared, too, if we got in the way.

"Jared busted loose as soon as he could. He'd stood up for Mom and me as much as he could, took some pretty hard knocks for us when Dad was at the bottom of the bottle. But when he had a way to get out, he took it, and I didn't blame him for it. I'd've joined too, but the military wasn't for me, and I knew it. Mom moved out with us when I was thirteen. Fourteen, maybe? Jared had just turned twelve, so yeah. I would've been fourteen. Filed for divorce. Of course, my dad still got visitation every other month, which was pretty fucked up, since he drank even more after we left. He didn't hit us when it was just us. He was always going after Mom. He'd get drunk and turn on some stupid kids' movie. *Bambi* or something. We didn't argue, just wait till he passed out and turn on something else. That was pretty much it. We'd see him twice a month, he'd buy us some crap, take us for ice cream. He finally figured out we hated the Disney movies, so he started playing movies Mom wouldn't let us watch. But we started getting older, and he just...he didn't know what to do with me."

"My brother has a daughter who's a teenager. Teenagers are difficult."

"Especially when you didn't want kids in the first place, like in our case."

"Oh, come on, Anna, I'm sure that's not—"

"I heard him say it, Jeff." I took a too-big swallow of wine and coughed. "I was listening out my window after Dad dropped Jared and me off, one Sunday night. He and Mom were arguing. Dad said he had to skip visitation for the next few weekends. Called it 'business.' Mom called it bull-shit. She wanted him to spend more time with us, and he kept making excuses. Eventually my mom badgered him into getting so pissed off he just admitted it. 'I never wanted kids, Laura!' is exactly what he said. Mom flipped the fuck out on him. I refused to see him after that. I guess I always knew he didn't want me, but to hear it…"

"That's a shitty thing to say."

"Yeah. He knew it, too. He saw me in my window, tried to explain how that's not what he meant, but—"

"But the damage was done." Jeff's eyes were full of compassion.

"Yeah. That was when I was fifteen. I didn't really see him except for a handful of times since. He died a couple years ago. Cirrhosis of the liver."

"What about your mom?"

I pinched the bridge of my nose. I hated talking about my parents. "Jeff, this is history. I hate—"

"It's important to me."

I finished the wine and spun the cup by the stem between my fingers. "God. Okay. Well, my mom is more complicated. I love her, I do. She raised me by herself after she and Dad split up, and she did the best she could. Then she met her new husband, Ed. She changed when she met him. I don't know even know what it is, exactly, but she's just...different. She was always high-strung, passionate and outspoken and all that—"

"Gee, I wonder why that's familiar," Jeff said, grinning.

"Yeah, I wonder," I laughed. "But when she met Ed and starting dating him, she got more... just bitchy. I can't explain it much better. She's just not as nice anymore. It's something to do with Ed. He's an okay guy, it's not like he's not a perv or a complete dickhead or anything. He's just—I don't know—passive aggressive? Never openly disagrees with you or does anything outright rude or insulting or whatever, but he just makes these little digs, so subtle you have to think about whether or not he actually insulted you. By the time you figure it out that you're pissed off about it, it's long past the time you can say anything."

Jeff grimaced. "Ugh. I had a lieutenant in the Army like that. Except when someone like that is your superior officer, it's even worse, because if he does insult you, you can't do dick about it."

"Yeah, see, my mom thinks Ed can do no wrong. She thinks he's like...mini-Jesus or something. I don't know. Mom and Ed have been married for, like, almost fifteen years."

"How old is Miri?" Jeff asked, after a brief pause in the conversation.

"Um...twenty-three? Twenty-four? I'm twenty-six, and she's a little over two years younger than me. So yeah, she'd be twenty-four. She got married to Kyle when she was twenty, just barely. Their twins, Eric and Dawson, are three. Why do you want to know all this?"

"You never answered me about whether twins run in your family," Jeff said.

I sighed. "I don't know. I think my paternal grandfather had a twin brother. My dad had siblings, but no twin that I'm aware of. So it might." I narrowed my eyes at Jeff. "Why does it matter?"

"Well, my brother has twin girls. So if it runs in both of our families, then if you and I ever had kids, there's a big likelihood we'd have twins."

"You're thinking about kids already?" Something like panic shot through me. "Jesus, Jeff. I haven't even fully processed that we're actually going to get married yet. Can we slow this down a tiny bit?"

Jeff didn't answer for a long moment. "It was just a thought, honey. I'm not saying I'm ready for kids, or trying to have a conversation about it. It was just a realization. If you have twins on your side, and I do mine, then its something we should be prepared for, if and when we're ready to start thinking about kids. That was my only point, I promise."

I let out a long breath. "I'm sorry, I guess I'm just feeling like things are moving a bit fast."

Jeff tangled his fingers in mine. "How so?"

"Just everything. Things with Chase over the last couple days really messed with my head, I think. You proposing was a surprise in itself. Now all that with Chase is settled, and suddenly we're engaged, which I'm happy about." I rubbed my thumb on his knuckle. "I don't want you to think I'm not happy or excited about this, Jeff. I am, I promise. It's just a lot, when a matter of weeks ago I wasn't even sure who I was really in love with. I'm overwhelmed, I guess."

"I guess that's understandable," Jeff said. "Things've been crazy for you lately."

"No kidding. I just...I want things to be normal for a hot minute. Just you and me. Let me get used to the idea of being engaged. It still doesn't feel real."

"I hear you. We'll give it time. No rush. We can plan when you're ready."

That sounded good to me.

Chapter 4

JEFF LET IT BE for about three months. We went out together, we worked. We made love. He never brought up the wedding, never asked me if I was ready to plan, or even dropped any hints.

I fell even harder in love with him for that. I knew it was on his mind. I could see it in his eyes when he looked at me, when he took my hand in his and touched my ring with his thumb.

I think maybe the first hint I was ready for wedding plans came when I realized I'd thought of the engagement ring on my finger as "my ring" as opposed to "his ring." It seems like a silly distinction, I guess, but it was an important one to me. No one had ever given me anything worth a lot of money. My cars had all been bought by me with money earned by me. I'd been given earrings and necklaces before, but nothing expensive or extravagant. We were spending a lot of time at his house, and as much as I was beginning to think of it as "home," it was still *his* house, not mine. My car was old and starting to break down from one thing after another, so Jeff would often have me drive his Yukon if I needed to go somewhere, but it was still *his* truck, not mine. I had *my* cell phone, *my* clothes.

So, to me, the ring on my finger—worth more than my car several times over, I was pretty certain—was his ring. A thing he'd bought and had given to me, to mark me as his. But it wasn't mine.

I was at the store, buying milk, bread, beer, frozen chicken breasts, feminine pads, razor heads, and hand soap. The cashier paused in the process of swiping and scanning my items to glance at my left hand, resting on the little ledge with the card reader. My ring glinted in the fluorescent lights, and the cashier, a tiny, awkward-looking woman with sharp features and oily brown hair, reached out and touched my hand near the ring.

"Wow, that is *gorgeous*!" she said, her wide, genuine smile showing nicotine-stained teeth.

I smiled at her, then glanced at my hand. "My ring? It is pretty, isn't it? Thanks."

My ring? The realization of what I'd just said hit me like a bolt of lightning. *Is it my ring? Or his?*

The cashier was speaking to me, but I didn't hear her.

It is my *ring, isn't it?*

I realized she was waiting for me to answer a question. "I'm sorry, what'd you say?"

"I asked when the wedding was?" She resumed scanning the last of my items and totaled it. "Forty-six eighty-two, please."

I counted out the cash, wondering what the correct answer was. We didn't have a date. We'd been engaged three months, and we had no date, no venue, no caterer, nothing.

"Um, we haven't set a date yet. We kinda just got engaged not too long ago," I said, eventually.

"Oh, well, congratulations, then."

"Thanks." I took my receipt and left, my head spinning.

I sat in Jeff's truck, the bags of groceries on the floor behind the passenger seat. Our groceries. Things for me, things for him, things for us. I was going to go home—to Jeff's house—and make dinner for us. I had half the closet full of my clothes. Space in the cabinet for my toiletries. Coats in the front closet. My phone charger in the kitchen.

I'd never lived with anyone before. Jeff hadn't asked me to officially move in, or made any comment about the mysterious influx of my things into his house, but my stuff seemed to suddenly have their own specific place in the house, and I found myself putting them there.

Jeff wasn't my boyfriend or my lover, or my fuck-buddy. He was my fiancé. I'd agreed to marry him. *Marry* him.

Sitting in the truck, *his* truck, I realized I'd only said yes because that seemed like the right answer. It was a way of making the decision between Jeff and Chase. It wasn't because I'd actually expected to get married, to have a wedding.

Get married. Have a wedding. The phrases rolled off the tongue easily enough, slipped through the mind quietly enough. But to put images to them, make them reality, that was different. Married meant only Jeff, for as long as I lived.

I tried the thought on: Anna Cartwright. Wife of Jeff Cartwright.

Hi, this is my husband Jeff.

My husband, Jeff.

Suddenly I saw flowers, lighting a candle, Jeff's hand on mine. Jeff sliding a ring, a simple band, on my finger. Jeff in a tuxedo.

Me, in a dress. All I could see of the dress, in my imagined fantasy, was waves of white, and my skin, and Jeff kissing me. Movie images, not reality images. But I could see it.

Where did you start planning a wedding? I had no idea.

I pulled out my phone and called the one person who might know. "Hey, Jay. So...if I was, hypothetically speaking, wanting to start planning a wedding, where would I start?"

Jamie was silent for a long time. "Um. I...don't know. I've never thought about getting married before. I'm not that kind of girl any more than you are."

"Yeah, so now you know my problem."

"Does Jeff know you're thinking about this?"

"No, I just now realized it."

"Oh. So...what happened that you're suddenly thinking about it for real?"

"It was weird. I'm at Meijer, grocery shopping. Well, I was, I'm in the car now, but...the cashier asked about my ring, and I realized I was thinking about it as *my* ring."

She got the significance of it immediately. "Oh. Wow."

"Yeah. Wow. And then I realized I was shopping for *us*. And I'm going to take the groceries *home*. To my *fiancé*. And it all just kind of sank in."

"Well, I think most girls start by looking at dresses. That's what they show on TV, at least. I don't know. That's where I'd say we start. Maybe it'll make it all seem more real, or whatever."

"What kind of dress do I get?" I wore skirts, and even a few full-length dresses every now and again. I mean, it's not like I'm a tomboy, wearing jeans and sweatshirts all the time. I'm a woman, and I like fashion as much as any other girl. I read *Cosmo* and *OK* and magazines like that. I like romantic comedies. But I don't know anything about wedding dresses.

Jamie laughed, but it was a confused, disbelieving laugh. "Well, how the hell should I know? It's not like I sit around watching *Say Yes to the Dress*."

"Do too. I've caught you watching it."

"That's a dirty lie. Take it back."

"The first step to recovery is admitting you have a problem."

I heard a blender in the background, and she sounded distant as if she was holding the phone between her shoulder and ear. "I'm not an addict. I can stop any time. It's just because I get so bored sometimes. All those long nights alone."

"You haven't spent more than three days alone at home in all the time I've known you."

"Shut up. So when are we going to look at wedding dresses, Miss 'I'm ready to get married finally'?"

"Tomorrow? Lunch and then we can go to…a wedding dress store. Somewhere."

Jamie was silent for a few beats. "I think you have to make an appointment. It's not like going to buy a new skirt."

"Oh. Well. I guess I'll have to Google wedding dress boutiques or whatever and make an appointment? Or maybe we can go and just look, at first. Kinda get our feet wet."

"Your feet, maybe. Mine are staying dry. And out of wedding dress shoes."

"That's what you say now. If I'm getting married, then so are you. Just watch."

"God, now you've gone and cursed me, you meddling bitch."

We laughed, more at each other than because anything was funny. "I'll call you when I know what the hell I'm going to do."

"'Kay, see you later."

"Jamie?"

"Yeah?"

"You're gonna be my maid of honor, right?"

Silence. "Um. Obviously. Unless you have a secret *other* best friend I don't know about." Jamie laughed to make it a joke, but I could tell she was emotional. "Except I'm not really a maid. I think you have to be a virgin to be a maid. Or at least, virtuous. So I'll be the skank of honor."

"You're not a skank."

"Yep. That's me. The skanky-ho of honor."

"Jamie, seriously."

"The horny slut of honor."

I sighed. Her self-deprecation wore on my patience sometimes, more frequently now than ever. I used to think it was just her way of joking, but I was beginning to think she was serious.

"Jay, knock it off. You're being stupid."

"Okay, fine. Whatever. Call me."

"Bye."

Jeff came out and took the bags from me, and we put things away in companionable silence. I leaned back against the kitchen counter, spinning my ring in circles, wondering how to start talking about it all.

"Spit it out," Jeff said, brushing a strand of hair away from my mouth with his finger.

"I'm ready," I said.

"You're ready?" Jeff watched me spin my ring around my finger. "Sure? I've been trying not to—"

"I know you have," I said, sliding my arms around his waist, "and I can't even begin to thank you for giving me time."

"So what made you ready?"

I explained what had happened at Meijer, and how I'd talked to Jamie in the parking lot.

Jeff frowned. "She's your best friend, and I get that. But I guess I wish you'd talked to me first."

"It's instinctive, on some level," I said. "Something big happens and I call Jamie, or tell her when she comes home. Except now this is more home than my apartment, but she's still my best friend and I tell her everything."

"I know. I'm just saying. I want to be the first person you call when something happens." He kissed my cheekbone. "I'm not saying you can't tell Jamie things. She's your friend and that's important. I'm not trying to take that away."

"I know. It'll take a while to adjust my thinking, I guess."

"So. Where do you wanna start?"

"Well, that's what Jamie and I were talking about. I think she and I are gonna go look at dresses."

"When?"

I set out the chicken to thaw and flipped through a cookbook, looking for something to make. "I don't know. Jamie says you need an appointment first, but I don't even know where those kinds of stores are. Bridal stores, dress boutiques, all that."

"Are you looking forward to it?"

I shrugged. "I don't know. It could be fun."

Jeff leaned against the counter next to me, flipping his phone in his hand. "So should I start looking for churches around here? Or do you want to do a destination wedding? We could do the Florida Keys. I have—"

"Lemme guess, an Army buddy," I said, still flipping pages but not really seeing anything.

Jeff laughed. "Yeah. I must be kinda predictable, huh? Well, anyway, yeah, my buddy Arnie has a house on the beach down there, lots of room. There's even a country club nearby Arnie's a member of, he could arrange for the reception to be held there."

I quit flipping pages and looked at Jeff. "Then everyone would have to travel down there to be at the wedding."

"Well, yeah, that's the point of a destination wedding. I'm pretty sure most everyone on my side wouldn't have a problem taking a few days, especially if we have it in the summer, when people take summer vacations anyway."

"Wouldn't it be crazy hot in Florida in the summer?"

"Late summer, then. Have it in the evening."

"I guess this means I have to actually decide about my mother, huh?"

Jeff glanced away, out the window, and then back at me, as if containing a subtle irritation. "Yeah, guess so. That's the real reason you didn't want to think about the wedding. Right?"

I nodded. "I can call my mom. Jared, too. Maybe he can get leave if we give him enough time. If we have it in Florida, Miri and Kyle and the boys can be there. Doubt they could take a vacation to anywhere far."

"I guess Florida sounds good. We can talk more later. Depends on Mom and Ed, though."

"All right."

I left Jeff sitting on the couch, staring at his jeans, picking at the dirt under his thumbnail, lost in thought.

"I don't know, Jamie. I'm not sure about this one. There's too much tulle and lace. It's not me."

Jamie tilted her head, biting the corner of her lower lip, eyebrows furrowed. "Yeah, you're right. It's too…frou-frou. Something simpler next."

I turned to the may-I-help-you person, a woman a few years older than I named Brandi, slim, with pale white skin and flaxen hair pulled into a high, severely tight ponytail.

She nodded. "I think I have something that might work. I'll bring it into the changing room."

Jamie and I went back to the changing room and Jamie helped me out of the dress.

"This is stressful," I said, adjusting the straps of my bra tighter. "Half of the dresses I try on I'm falling out of, the other half make my ass look huge. And the rest are ugly."

"That doesn't make any mathematical sense," Jamie said, hanging the old dress up.

"Shut up. It doesn't have to. I thought trying on wedding dresses was supposed to be fun."

"It is. You're just difficult. And the only dress that made your ass look big was the mermaid one."

I snorted a laugh. "That didn't make my ass look big, it made it look like my ass had its own damn zip code. Which I'm starting to think it does."

Jamie smacked my shoulder. "Shut up, hooker. Your ass does not have a zip code. It doesn't even have an address, 'cause our lease just ran out."

"Don't remind me. Are we renewing?"

Jamie shrugged, fidgeting with the dress on the hanger, studiously avoiding my gaze. "Why would we? You're getting married in a few months. You should just move in with Jeff now. Save yourself the trouble after the honeymoon. 'Sides, you already live there half the time anyway."

I let my hair out of the ponytail and retied it to get the strays off my neck. "Then what will you do?"

She still wouldn't look at me. "I don't know. I'll figure it out. Not your problem."

"You're my best friend. Of course it's my problem."

Brandi came in then, effectively ending the conversation. "I think you might like this. It's A-line, just a touch of lace around the hem and the bust. It's simpler than the others you've tried on, but I think it'll look lovely on you. I think the bust line will nicely accentuate your full figure."

I winced. *Full figure*. Means plus-size. Curvy. Voluptuous. More euphemisms for not size-zero.

Brandi noticed my reaction and touched my shoulder, stammering. "I—I mean—"

"What she means is, you've got great tits," Jamie cut in, "and this will make 'em look even better. Jeff won't be able to take his eyes off your boobs."

Brandi breathed a soft sigh of relief when I laughed, and then she turned to hang the dress on the hook and pull it out of the bag. I stepped into it, and Brandi helped me adjust it to my full-figure boobs and zip it up the back. I hadn't looked at myself in the mirrors as I got into the dress, and I wasn't sure I wanted to yet. This dress felt nice. It felt...comfortable. Not heavy or draggy like some, or too light and airy like others. I could feel a lot of skin bare to the air, and I knew, even without looking, that my breasts would indeed be on display in a big way. Jeff would like that, but I wasn't sure I wanted to look like a hooker or pinup girl.

I tugged the cups higher, stuffed my boobs deeper in, breathed deeply and let it out. I glanced at Jamie first, to get her reaction. She had her hand clamped over her mouth, and her eyes were shimmering.

Oh, shit. She's crying.

I closed my eyes, turned back to the mirrors, and then looked at myself. My eyes stung, suddenly burning. Jamie came up next to me and tugged my hair back out of the ponytail, fluffed it out, and then pulled a bobby pin from her own hair and pinned my bangs behind my head, leaving the rest loose around my shoulders. Her eyes were wet, tears flowing freely now.

"God, Anna. You look...incredible."

"You really do," Brandi said, setting a veil attached to a tiara on my head and arranging the gauzy white material around my shoulders. "You look gorgeous."

I sniffed hard, ran my finger underneath my eyes.

I didn't look at myself in the mirror too often. I did my makeup, of course, but I leaned close and didn't really look at the rest of me. Clothes shopping wasn't something I did frequently, since I always felt like I had for most of the wedding dress shopping experience of the last few weeks: insecure about my body, overwhelmed by all the different kinds of dresses, stressed about having to choose *one* dress out of thousands.

But this…was different. All the other times I'd tried on dresses I'd looked at myself and seen my belly, or my wide hips, or the bulge of my ass, or my arms, or my *full figure* bust line. I didn't see me as a bride, I saw a girl in a wedding dress. A girl playing dress-up.

This time, though, when I opened my eyes and looked at myself in the mirror, even before Jamie fixed my hair and Brandi put on the veil, I felt like a bride. I felt…beautiful.

For the first time in a long time, I really looked at myself. I saw a tall woman, a few inches shy of six feet, long dyed-blonde hair wavy and loose around my bare shoulders, full breasts displayed but not spilling out. I saw my eyes, hazel and wavering with unshed tears within a heart-shaped face, high cheekbones, and full lips. I didn't see a dress size or a bust line or an ass that went on forever.

I saw me: curvy and confident. I saw a woman with a body made for loving, hands made for holding, lips meant for kissing. I saw wide, expressive eyes and blush-pink cheeks. I saw me as Jeff might see me. I saw the body that gave him a hard-on just looking at it, naked and wet from the shower. I saw the woman he loved, the woman he desired.

I saw the woman he wanted to marry. No longer a girl playing dress-up, or a girl in a wedding dress, or an insecure plus-size girl.

I saw me, beautiful the way I am.

Jamie touched my eyes with a Kleenex and rested her chin on my shoulder. "This one?" I could only nod and try to hold back the tears. "I'm pretty sure you're supposed to cry when you find the dress," Jamie said.

I shook my head, refusing to let them fall. I was happy. I was overwhelmed. I wasn't going to cry.

"Anna. It's fine."

I shook my head again and swiped my finger underneath each eye. "I'm fine. Really. I just—"

"It's overwhelming," Brandi said, standing near the door. "You see yourself in The Dress, and you finally realize it's really real. Like, it's actually going to happen. The veil is what usually does it for most of my clients."

"That's it exactly," I said. "Until now getting married was just an idea. But now...I can actually see myself walking down the aisle."

"Better you than me, girl," Jamie said, fidgeting with the veil.

"That's what I always thought," I said. "But now that I'm ready for it...I'm getting kind of excited."

"I'm happy for you. Really. I can't wait to be in the wedding. You and Jeff are perfect together. But it's not happening for me. No way, no how. Never."

"You're impossible."

"Yep."

"So when you do end up getting married, I get to say 'I told you so,' right?"

Jamie laughed. "If it happens, which it won't, then sure."

"So is this the dress, then?" Brandi asked.

"Yeah, I think so," I said, my voice wavering. I looked at myself once more, head to toe, and this time my voice had conviction. "Yes. This is the dress."

It would clean out the savings I'd been setting aside for a new car, and probably max out my credit card to boot, but it was worth it. Jamie and I met Jeff for lunch after making an appointment to return for a fitting.

Jeff had already ordered for us and was waiting at a four-top table at Five Guys. "So, how'd dress shopping go today?"

He'd never come with us, obviously, but he always wanted to know what was happening.

"I found the dress," I said, sitting next to him.

Jamie took the spot opposite me. "It's gorgeous," she said. "Like, incredible. You just might faint when you see her for the first time."

"I'm sure I will," Jeff said.

"No, really. All the blood's gonna rush to your cock and you're gonna pass out. It's that sexy."

"Jamie, seriously? You're incorrigible." I threw a French fry at her head.

"What? It's true. I'm a girl and I got a hard-on."

"Ohmigod, Jamie. You're so freaking impossible."

"You know you love it."

"True. But seriously, though, Jeff. I really love it." I dabbed a fry in ketchup. "My credit card balance doesn't love me, but it's worth it."

"How much was it?" Jeff asked.

"You don't want to know."

"*An*na. You can't go broke trying to do everything on your own."

"Neither can you."

"Anna."

I dabbed another fry. "Fivethousanddollars," I mumbled the words, all squished together and under my breath, and followed it with a bite of cheeseburger.

"Excuse me?" Jeff leaned forward, setting his burger down. "It sounded like you said five thousand dollars for a second there."

"Wow, I really like this song. I haven't heard it since the nineties," I said. "This is Gin Blossoms, right?"

"Anna."

"Fine. Yes. It was five thousand three hundred and ninety two dollars, okay?"

"You spent fifty-five hundred dollars?" Jeff sank back in his chair. "Good lord. I thought you'd at least call me before you went and blew your entire savings. I could have helped you. We're doing this together. At least, that was the idea."

"Are you really pissed off about this? I wanted to. It was what I wanted. I'm finally getting into this, getting into the whole 'planning a wedding' thing, and now you're pissed off that I made a decision. You're not supposed to see the dress until the actual wedding anyway."

"I know that, but we could have split the difference or something. At least talk to me before you go and spend that much money. I thought that's what couples did?"

"Well, shit. I'm sorry I didn't consult you first. I guess I thought I was old enough to make my own decisions."

"That's not what I meant—"

"Wow, look at that soda dispenser," Jamie said, a little too loudly, getting up for a refill. "They have like, a dozen different kinds of Fanta."

"Jeff, let it go."

"Well, at least call your—"

"If you bring up my mother, I will straight up walk out. For real. I am *not* calling her to help pay for my wedding."

"Didn't you want your mom to be there when you picked your dress? It's kind of traditional, isn't it?"

"Jeff, you really need to stop pushing this family button, okay? Yeah, maybe it is traditional, but Jamie is more my family than my mom at this stage. Tradition can jump off a cliff. I just want a happy wedding. I don't want my family there. Just you and me and those who really matter. My blood family doesn't matter. Not anymore."

"I know I'm pushing it, but...it's important to me. Family is important to me."

"You're my family. Jamie is my family."

"What about Jared?" Jeff picked at the Cajun-seasoned fries.

"Well, he's been in the Marines since I was, like, twenty, and he's only spent his leave Stateside, like, three times, ever, so I don't see him at all. He'll message me using the TextMe app every now again, but that's it."

"Where's he stationed?"

"The Philippines. He's been there for...three years? He was in Okinawa first, then Italy."

"What's his MOS?"

"He's an MP."

Jamie had come back to the table but had pretended to be absorbed in her phone. "He's hot. If he lived here, Anna and I would be sisters."

"I thought that was never happening, with anyone."

"For your sexy-ass brother, I might make an exception." She looked up at me and saw my irritated expression. "God, Anna. Kidding. I would never marry Jared. I'd fuck him till he couldn't walk for a week, though."

"JAMIE!"

"Shutting up."

We finished eating, and Jamie and I said our goodbyes. I promised to call her with the next step of our plans. Jeff drove us home, but before we went inside, Jeff spoke up: "So, this dress you picked out."

"You can't see it until I'm walking down the aisle."

"No, I know that, but—"

"You want to know how I knew which dress was the right one?"

"Yeah."

"I saw myself like you see me. Just for a second, looking in the mirror. I saw the woman you love, the woman you want." I paused. "Would it be overly dramatic if I said it was kind of a defining moment in my life?"

"Really?"

"Yeah, really. To finally, finally feel my own worth in myself...I can't explain how huge that is for me. Not just through you, or through Chase. But in myself. Actually *seeing* with my own eyes a woman worth being. Yes, it was a defining moment of my life."

"And I shit all over it, freaking out about the money."

I laughed. "Yeah, you kind of did. But I get it. You couldn't have understood if I didn't tell you. I don't care how much the dress costs. I'd sell my liver if it meant feeling that way again. And yeah, I know it's just one day. I don't care. If you want to pay for it, or split the cost, fine. Whatever. I really do want to do this with you. I'm just...I'm not used to being a couple. To doing things like that together. But I want to."

Jeff's deep brown eyes swept over my face, love radiating from him in palpable waves. "Thanks for telling me."

"I would've eventually. I just—"

"Needed a little prodding," Jeff said.

"Yeah."

"I'm pretty good at prodding," he said, a mischievous smirk on his face.

"Hmmm. I might have to test your prodding abilities. You know. To make sure they're up to expectation. We have very strict prodding standards, you know."

"What kind of test did you have in mind?" he asked, feigning curiosity.

"Come inside and I'll show you," I said.

His eyes lit up with a lustful hunger as we went inside.

"Take me," I gasped, my lips against the hair above his ear. "Take me right here, right now."

Lately, we'd gotten into a pattern. We'd work, go back to his place, have a glass of wine or a bottle of beer, and then go into his room, our room, and make love. It was a pattern I enjoyed. There were nights we simply went to sleep, holding each other. The sex, even when it was the same basic thing or two every night, was never stale, never boring. I could see us in ten years, still enjoying vanilla missionary sex just as much as now.

But this, the fiery hunger flickering in Jeff's eyes, the demanding way he pinned me back against the front door and chained my wrists by my face with his strong hands, this was sudden and powerful and lit me from within. He didn't kiss me at first. He held my hands in his, palm against palm, fingers lined up, his dwarfing mine. Then, slowly, he curled his fingers into mine, clenching tight. His lips explored my mouth, his tongue pushing between my lips to taste my tongue.

I kissed him with eyes wide open, watching his expression change moment by moment: lust, love, hunger, need, raw and potent strength. He circled both of my wrists with one hand, holding them up over my head. With his other he lifted my shirt up, stripped it off, releasing my hands long enough to pull it free and toss it aside. His mouth dipped to my shoulder, kissed the round bend from shoulder to arm, then upward to my neck, my jaw. Gentle, nimble fingers unclasped my bra, dropped it to my feet. While my hands were free to slip the straps off my arms, I tried to wrap my arms around his neck, but he caught my wrists again and pinned them above my head, kissing me with startling power.

I melted into the kiss, relaxed into his hold, pressed my bare breasts against the rough cotton of his button-down shirt. His free hand traced down my side, butted against the waist of my jeans and circled around to the front, toying with the button before releasing it. He lowered himself down, stretching his arm to keep my hands in place, his lips kissing a hot, moist line down my chest and between my breasts. He tugged my pants down, one side at a time until they pooled at my feet, and then he repeated the action with my panties.

My back was still against the front door, my heart thudding with anticipation. This was a new, demanding Jeff, in control and taking what he wanted from me. Excitement made my hands tremble and my lips shake against his, and when his teeth grazed my nipple, wet heat burst between my thighs. I struggled against his hold, wanting to touch him, needing to strip him down to skin and slide my legs around him.

He held me still, crushing me against the door with his body, kissing me with hard fury. His mouth demanded my acquiescence, and I gave it, opening to him, softening against him. When I was still and only our lips moved against each other, he leaned back and ripped his shirt open, buttons popping and ticking on the floor at our feet, then, with the fabric dangling from his arm, he deftly slipped out of his pants so he was naked in front of me.

I expected him to push me to our bedroom then, but he didn't. He pressed burning kisses around my breasts, focusing in on one and laving the nipple, circling it, nipping it. His free hand slid palm against my belly, fingers pointing down and moving between my thighs. He cupped me, and I whimpered, wanting to feel his fingers delve in, but he drew out for the moment, smiling against my lips.

"Tell me what you want, Anna," he whispered, his voice a rough, primal growl in the silent, evening-lit house.

"You," I answered, pushing my pussy against his hand, willing him to touch me.

He rewarded me with a single fingertip slipping between my nether lips.

"Tell me more. What else do you want?"

I bent my head down to rasp my answer in his ear, "Put your finger inside me. Make me come, Jeff."

He growled, a rolling animal sound of hunger. His finger dipped in, sought my juices and slathered them over my soft folds, finding the hard nub of my clit and softly swiping around it. I moaned and rolled with his moving finger, pushing my breasts against his bare chest.

"Yes, just like that," I said, "two fingers, now. Yes, god yes. Faster."

He obeyed my commands, moving faster until I almost couldn't stand it.

"Slower, slower. Slow down." I let myself fade away from the ragged edge of orgasm, until his fingers were barely moving against me. "Faster, not so hard. Soft. Yes, just like that. Oh, god, Jeff. I love the way you touch me."

Climax rose slowly, this time. I let it build gradually. My arms were starting to tingle over my head, but I ignored it.

"Put your mouth on my tits," I said. "Suck my nipples."

"Yes," was his only response.

His lips found one nipple, then the other, his fingers circling my clit. I opened my mouth to tell him to slow down, but then climax hit me without warning, gushing through me, ripping the strength from my knees. I collapsed, shuddering, and only Jeff's hand held me aloft.

Jeff's knee nudged my thighs apart, and I forced myself upright on trembling legs. I felt his hard tip brush against my thigh as he crouched and rose up. Gently, slowly, carefully, he guided himself into me. When our hips bumped and his cock filled me, I felt my legs go limp again, and I was held up by him, by his hands around my wrists and his cock within me.

I curled over him, my face against his shoulder, bit his salty skin. He gasped at the sharp nip, and then thrust into me, once, hard, and my whimper of pleased shock was muffled by his flesh. I was lifted up onto my toes, and then he was fading out and plunging back in, pressed back against the door by the power of his body coursing against mine. I let my weight fall against him, trusting his strength. The climax, still rocking through me, redoubled, inundating me with searing ecstasy. I let my voice rise in volume, giving in to the pleasure, shrieking and gasping as he began to drive into me with ever greater force.

His hand released mine and I wrapped my arms around his neck, clinging to him. He slid his hands beneath my ass and lifted me. I wrapped one leg around his waist, and he held it there, rocking up on his toes to crush ever deeper.

"Jeff..." I could only gasp his name as the waves of orgasm trebled in intensity, each crest indecipherable from the one before or behind. I squeezed my eyes shut and rode the climax, gasping with each surge of his body against me, the pitch

of my voice rising until I was screaming unabash-
edly, back arched, face thrown to the ceiling, hips
gyrating madly.

I felt him come, heard his bellow. His cock
throbbed, pulsed, and released a flood of seed
within me, hot and washing through me. His face
buried in my breasts, he groaned as he came again,
and again, moving his body into me in sinuous
thrusts.

I hadn't thought I could come any harder without breaking apart at the seams, and yet I did, feeling him spasm and arch into me, feeling him lose
himself in me.

"God, I love you," I whispered in the silence
between our breaths.

"You're my eternity, Anna."

Tears dripped from me, a sudden rush of hot
salt burning my cheeks. "Fuck. You've gone and
made me cry after sex again."

"Good tears?"

"Good tears."

"Cry if you want. Doesn't bother me." He let
me down, pulled out, and we lay on the couch,
pulling a hand-knit afghan over us.

I was messy, and I didn't care. "I've cried so
much lately. I don't know what it is."

"You're finally learning to feel your emotions?"

"Yeah, maybe." I nuzzled my face into his
broad shoulder. "I just wish there weren't so many
of them. I feel like a basket case sometimes."

"I love who you are, and I love every single thing about you, good or bad. I know you've been through some hard shit, and I wish I could take away the pain you've carried. I would take it on myself if I could. But I wouldn't change anything about you. Our pain and mistakes and faults are an integral part of us. They make our joy and successes and qualities all the more significant."

"That's...deep."

"Sit with a gun staring at nothing for days on end, you tend to have a lot of time to think."

"You know, all I really know about that is you were in the Army. I don't know for how long, or what you did, or if...if you saw combat."

"Yeah, don't talk about that much." He seemed to stiffen, his muscles tensing.

I waited, curled into him on the couch, my hand resting low on his belly.

"Not a whole lot to say, really. Saw combat. It was fucked up. Things you shouldn't see, shouldn't do." His words were clipped short, his voice barely audible.

I looked up at him, saw his closed eyes flickering, as if seeing the past.

"If it's too hard to talk about—"

"It's more that there's no point. It's not like I'm super hung up on it. I had PTSD counseling, I'm over it. Few bad dreams here and there." He looked down at me and drew a breath, let it out.

"Here's the basics. I was a grunt. Infantryman. Did a tour in Iraq. God, it was fucking boring as hell for the most part. A whole lot of sitting on a roof watching dust blow around. Drive here and there in a Hummer, house-to-house patrols. My unit got ambushed, toward the middle of my tour. It was a pretty standard insurgent ambush. Lead vehicle hit a land mine, and when the others stopped, they opened fire. Lost some good buddies in that one. My nightmares are usually about that. Haven't had one in a while. So, if you wake up and I'm not in bed, that's why. I'll probably be outside in the backyard. Fresh air helps."

I heard an odd note in his voice. "What aren't you saying?"

"Perceptive one, aren't you?" He scrubbed his face with his hand. "My vehicle got hit by an RPG. They kinda missed, you know? Hit near it, not dead on, but enough to...well, no one made it out alive, 'cept me. Not sure why I made it, or how. I was trapped in the back seat, the whole thing burning, buddies dead, buddies dying outside. Taking heavy fire from all directions. That's the dream. It's more a memory, being trapped in a burning vehicle."

"Was this before or after the car wreck in the UP?" I asked.

He grunted. "Before. That's the reason I went nuts trying to save Brett. He was trapped. Like I'd been. Had to do something, *had to*. But I couldn't save him." A long silence, then, "So now you know. Never really talked about that before."

"How'd you get out? Of the vehicle, I mean?"

"Couple guys heard me yelling. Screaming, more like. Pulled me out, and we used the wreck as cover. Wicked enfilade fire. Couldn't see where they were shooting from. Hidden in a bombed-out building, a good fifty of 'em. We were almost double their numbers, but they had surprise. Took us a while to get organized. When we did, though... wiped 'em out. Every last fucking one."

He slid out from behind me, strode naked to the sliding glass door. I gave him a few minutes, just lay on the couch watching him. Eventually, I got up, wrapped the afghan around me, and stood behind him, palms on his chest. His heart was hammering in his chest.

"I'm sorry I brought up bad memories, Jeff."

He took a few long, deep breaths. "It's fine. I'll be fine. Just takes a bit for the memories to fade, you know? But they will."

"Want a drink?"

He shook his head. "No, not yet. One thing the counselor emphasized a lot was, when the memories are riding you, don't turn to alcohol. That's how it becomes a crutch. It seems natural enough. Bad dream? Have a drink. But the memories hold on, you know? They stick. And one drink turns to four. Turns to eight. Turns to passed out on the

bathroom floor. Saw it happen to too many buddies to let it happen to me."

"I'm proud of you," I said.

"Proud? For what?" He turned his head so he
could just barely see me in his peripheral vision.

"For dealing with it so well. I would never have
known you'd been through anything so awful. I
think a lot of men would have been bitter, or alco-
holics. Or, I don't know. Just, I'm proud of you.
You're so strong."

He shook his head. "Lots of guys have been
through shit like that. Not all of them turn to drugs
or alcohol. A lot of us are normal, well-adjusted
men with normal, well-adjusted lives. We just…
have some bad memories that haunt us sometimes.
Women like you, who understand and help us deal,
you're how we get through the flashbacks and stay
sane."

"I haven't done anything, though. Not yet, at
least."

"You listened. You're here, holding me. Talking
to me."

"Well, what else would I do?"

"You haven't asked the one question almost
everyone wants to know, whether they ask it out
loud or not: 'Did you kill anyone?'"

I let the pause hang. "I…guess I'm not sure why
I'd ask. It's obviously hard for you to think about.
I don't want you reliving it. I mean, I'm assuming

since you said you saw combat, that you probably did."

"Exactly." He turned and put his back to the glass. "Enough about the bad old days. Come here and kiss me."

And so I did. I welcomed the distraction from my own memories, and the opportunity to help erase the pain in his eyes, to fill the haunted hollowness. I kissed him with all I had. I let the blanket fall to the floor and ran my hands on the ridges of his muscle, the ropy cords of strength in his arms and abs. I ran my fingers along the rough, burned skin along his back, so familiar to my touch now that I forgot it was there, what it was, what it represented. It was simply a part of Jeff, an element of his attractiveness to me.

I felt his body respond, stiffening and standing up between us; I took his manhood in my hands and caressed his length, softly, gently, with as much tenderness as I could summon. When he was throbbing between my palms, I released him and led him, walking backward, to the bedroom. I pushed him onto the bed and climbed astride him. My hair fell in blonde waves around our faces as I leaned down to kiss him, taking his turgid cock in my hand and guiding his hard length into my soft, wet cleft. My mouth quivered wide in an open-mouthed kiss as he penetrated me.

Our bodies glided in synchronized splendor, skin sliding slick and soft, our breath a slow susurrus in the dusk light. I moved on top of him, ran my palms on his chest up to cup his face, kissing him on the offbeat, lips touching in a syncopated rhythm. He'd given it to me hard and fast and sudden against the front door; now I was giving it to him slow and locked in melodic counterpoint of soul expression, eyes meeting, closing, meeting, hips bumping and pulling away, gasps turning to sighs.

This was not about climax. I felt his tension fade with every thrust, felt his memories sink into nothingness with every soft kiss. I couldn't heal him, but I could douse the heat of the nightmare, subsume the horror beneath the power of my love.

When it came, it was a tidal wave, sweeping us away. He clung to me as if I were a spar and he a shipwrecked sailor. He moved into me with a desperation unlike anything I'd ever seen in him before, as if he could bury the nightmare memories within me, be free of them forevermore simply through the act of driving deeper into me.

If that was true, I would accept it all.

His breath caught when he came, and a single sob escaped his lips. I kissed each of his cheeks, the single trickle of salt at each corner. I asked no questions, spoke no words, only held him closer and pushed him deeper within my folds, clutching his face against mine, forehead to forehead, breathing matched and his legs tangled with mine.

In time, we found a perfect stillness, contentedness in breathing, holding, being. Loving. I leaned over to kiss him and tasted salt on his lips, moisture on his face. I wiped his cheek with my palm, then the other.

"Sorry," he muttered, gruff, moving to sit up. "I don't know why I'm—"

"Shh. Don't." I pushed him down and kissed him again. "You're allowed."

He went still, and after a while he cleared his throat and brushed his palms across his face. "Thanks," he said. "I guess I just—"

"I know. I love you. Like I said, you're allowed. Doesn't make you less a man...less my man."

"And that's why I love you. Well, one of the infinite number of reasons, at least. Now, how 'bout that drink?"

Chapter 5

A FEW DAYS LATER, I had just gotten out of an afternoon shower and was looking for a particular bottle of body lotion. I tore the bathroom and bedroom apart, but couldn't find it, which was when I realized I'd never brought that particular bottle of lotion over to Jeff's house. It was still at my apartment, which I hadn't stepped foot in for at least a month. Half of my clothes, most of my makeup, hair products, lotions, all that "girly shit," as Jeff called it, was at his house. But every once in a while I came across something I wanted that turned out to be at my apartment.

This is ridiculous, I thought.

I found Jeff out on his back porch, reading a book on his Paperwhite. He looked up when I came out.

He took one look at my face as I approached and set his Kindle down. "What's up, buttercup? You look like you're thinking deep thoughts."

I handed him one of the bottles. "Well, just sort of wondering something."

"Wait, can I guess what you're about to say?"

"Um, sure?"

He reached into his pocket and pulled out a single key. "This is more symbolic than anything, since you're basically living here already, but..." He handed me the key. "Wanna make it official? Move in for real, permanently?"

I took the key and blew out a sigh of relief. "The idea of asking had me in knots." I frowned. "I've been paying my half of the rent with Jamie still, because I know she can't afford it on her own. The lease ran out, and we've going on a month-to-month basis. That's the part I'm really not sure of. What is she going to do?"

"Have you talked to her about it?" Jeff asked, picking at the peeling label of his bottle.

"Sort of. Not really. It came up while I was try-ing on dresses, but not since. She's been my best friend and roommate forever. I'll miss her, but I also worry about her by herself." I took a long pull on my beer.

"She's a grown woman, Anna. She can take care of herself. She's not your responsibility. I know her

well enough to know she'd kick your ass for thinking that way."

"I know. You're right. But I can't help it. It's
not that I don't think she can take care of herself.
She's even more hard-headedly independent than I
am. She's a tough-ass. She'd never ask for help, or
take it if it was offered. It's more emotionally. She's
got damage, like me. Bad history. I just worry that
she's unhappy and can't get out of the rut she's in."

"Well, look at it like this: What can you do
about it, practically speaking, even if you were to
keep living with her?"

"Not much, I guess. If she wasn't ready to talk
about it, she wouldn't talk about it. She can be
prickly like that."

Jeff nodded, pulling the label free and shred-
ding it. "I've gotten glimpses of that. Just talk to
her. Tell her you're moving in with me, and what
your worries are. Be honest."

"Yeah, you're right. Thanks."

He smiled. "Of course, my love. "

I called Jamie the next day, and we met for
coffee.

When we had plunked ourselves down in the
big red chairs, I plunged right in. "I'm officially
moving in with Jeff. We talked about it last night."

Jamie gave an extravagant sigh and eye-roll.
"*Finally*. You've been pussyfooting it around that
for weeks. About damn time."

"I thought you'd be, I don't know…"

"Hey, you're my best friend. Living with you has been awesome. But we both knew it was coming. You're barely there as it is, and I'm not there much more myself. I've picked up hours at work, and I've been seeing this new guy, so that's kept me busy—"

I snickered. "I'll bet it has."

"Like you have room to talk, hooker."

"Hey, mine put a ring on it," I said.

She lifted a skeptical eyebrow. "Haven't we already talked about this? I don't want a ring. I'm happy being the booty call. No-strings sex all the way, baby."

I left the pause hanging. "Are you really?"

Jamie slid the cardboard sleeve of her white paper cup off and on, not meeting my eye. "How about them Tigers, huh?"

"Jay. Seriously."

"Damn it, Anna. I so do *not* want to talk about this. I've already told you how I feel. I'm not marriage material. I'm good in bed, I'm fun to drink with, and I can give a killer blow job. But I can't cook for shit, I don't do laundry, and I hate compromise."

"Jay, listen. I'm not married yet, so I can't say for sure, but unless something magical happens when you say 'I do,' getting married is just a way of publicly binding yourself to one guy. It's not an indentured servitude contract. No guy should expect you to cook and clean and all that shit, unless that's the way you want your relationship. Some people are happy with the more traditional roles. I'm a foodie, so I like cooking. But I hate cleaning, and Jeff's a neat freak. He does most of the cleaning around his house—our house. I just do enough to keep him from getting irritated with me. It's all about finding someone who gets you. Everything else is up to you and him, and what you want your relationship to be."

"So how is with Jeff and you?"

"I don't know. It just is. We never really sat down and laid out the parameters of our relationship. We just…found a rhythm. He gets up at, like, five every morning out of habit from being in the Army. He goes to the gym and showers and all that before I've even gotten out of bed. I'm a monster in the mornings, and he's discovered that, so he gives me space. I didn't tell him, he just figured it out for himself. I realized it absolutely drives him batshit when I leave clothes on the bathroom floor, so I had to make myself stop doing it. He wouldn't say anything to me—he'd just clean up after me and had this way of making me feel guilty without ever really trying. I don't know how he does it."

"You make it work." She still wasn't looking at me. "That sounds great. I just can't see myself wanting to spend that much time around one person, all the time. Every day, every night. I don't know. The idea sounds nice, someone to count on, who knows me and stuff. But I've got skeletons in my closet, you know? Trusting someone with all that, it's scary."

"Hell, yeah it is," I said. "But it's worth it, if you decide to really trust him."

"How do you know you trust Jeff? I mean, if things don't work out, you'd be up shit creek, you know?"

"He knew about Chase. He let me go, and took me back. He made me work for his trust again after that, and I know, beyond a shadow of a doubt, if I ever messed up with another guy, Jeff would walk. It'd be done. And I know he's the one—as corny as that phrase is—because the idea of losing him makes my blood freeze. I get literally sick to my stomach at the thought of losing Jeff."

"Really?" Jamie was finally looking at me, and I could tell she was really listening, and thinking.

"Yeah, really. He's...part of me. I mean, he's been in my life as a friend and business partner for so long that it just seems like an extension of every-thing to be together." I gave Jamie a long, serious look. "And honestly, sex is only a part of it. Don't get me wrong, sex is, like, vital. But it's not every-thing. If he doesn't love you, it ends up being flat and empty."

"Meaningful sex? Gag." Jamie forced a laugh. "Kidding. I—fuck. I *do* want that, Anna. I do. I really, really do. I just don't know how to find it."

I considered my next words carefully. "I think...I think the trick is, love finds you. The harder you look, the more elusive it is. But when you finally give up and learn to be content just being you, *bam*, you're in love with last person you'd thought possible. And you can't fight it. Love is like quicksand—the harder you struggle against it, the deeper you fall in."

"Listen to you, all deep and wise like Confucius or some shit."

"I'm pretty sure Confucius never talked about falling in love."

"Okay, fine. Nicholas Sparks, then."

"Gag."

Jamie made an odd face. "Hey, he's actually a good writer. Don't knock him. *The Notebook* is ridiculously fucking adorable. Makes me all teary and pathetic."

I stared at her like she'd sprouted a second head. "You've read a Nicholas Sparks book?"

"What? I can read."

I laughed. "Well I know *that*, stupid. I just can't picture you curled up on the couch reading a book like that. Did you drink chamomile tea and dab your eyes meaningfully with a folded Kleenex, too?"

"You're being mean."

"I'm sorry, it's just a funny picture. You're not the Nicholas Sparks type, Jay. You're just not. You watch things with subtitles, and explosions and sex."

"What? I can't have a softer side?"

Her averted gaze told me she wasn't playing around anymore. "Of course you can, Jay. Look, I'm sorry. I didn't mean to suggest you *couldn't* be that kind of girl. I just haven't seen that side of you before. Honestly, I'm glad to hear you say that. I worry about you, sometimes."

"You worry about me? Why?"

"Just…you're so self-deprecating all the time. You've always got these boy-toys that never really go anywhere or mean anything, and I worry you think you're not…I don't know, worthy, or capable of anything more."

"What are you, a mind reader?" Her voice was too small, too quiet.

"Seriously?"

"Not all the time. There are days where I like who I am and think there's a lot I could offer a guy. But then there's other times where I doubt myself. That's usually when I'm doing the walk of shame at six a.m." She fidgeted with a button on her sweater.

"Jamie, you can't think that way. You're amazing, and beautiful—"

"What are you, my girlfriend? Save the pep talk, hooker. I know what I am. I'll find Mr. Right eventually. That's not your problem. It's mine." She pointed at me, jabbing her forefinger at me. "Your only worry should be getting married to your Mr. Right."

"Okay, just promise me one thing?"

"No guarantees, but I'll try."

"Dump your current booty call. Go without sex for a while. No boys. No kissing, no BJs, no hand jobs, nothing."

"God, you make it sound like I'm—"

"I'm just covering all the bases," I said. "I'm for real. No boys. Take some time to learn how to be single, how to just be you. Stop trying to fill the hole and just be you."

"I'm not sure I can do that," she said.

"Yes, you can."

"I haven't been truly single in…longer than I'm willing to admit out loud."

"Exactly. Okay, are you ready for another Confucius saying?"

"Hit me up."

"Empty sex is like Pringles: You can eat million of them, but they never really fill you up. If you want to be truly satisfied, you have to eat real food."

"No more one-night stands, is what you're saying."

"No more two- or three- or four-night stands. No more two-week stands. No more two-month stands. No stands at all. Stop looking. Stop trying. Someday, probably sooner than you think, a guy will come along, and you won't be able to stop thinking about him. It will go beyond wanting his hot body—it'll be about him, the man. And when that happens, wait to have sex until you can't wait anymore. Until you feel like you're going to die if you don't have him right the hell now."

"Anna, I—"

I grabbed her hands and squeezed as hard as I could. "Shut up and promise me, Jamie."

"I don't make promises. They only get broken." She stared at the floor between her feet.

"*Promise me.*"

She met my eyes. "This is really important to you?"

"Yes."

"Fine, then. But only because it's you. I promise."

"I'm serious about this."

"Yes, Anna. I said I promise. I'll go celibate. I promise."

"Okay, then."

"How did you come to this? I mean, it's not like you did it."

"If I hadn't found Jeff, I would have."

She frowned. "He was always right there."

"I know, but…I still found him. Found the real him, the one who'd been hiding from me until I was ready to really see him."

"When did you get so wise all of a sudden?"

I shrugged. "I don't know. I think it started with Chase. Realizing I was beautiful, and worth loving…it did something to me."

"You found your softer side."

I nodded. "Exactly. What I really want is for you to explore yours, and I don't think you will if you've got a boyfriend to distract you."

"I know what you mean. I will. I promise." She made a shooing motion with her hands. "Now, enough about me. Go plan your wedding."

My dress was ready a little more than two weeks later. It had fit almost perfectly in the store, so it hadn't needed much. I picked it up and brought it home.

Home. It hadn't taken much to move me completely into Jeff's house. I didn't have much by way of furniture, and most of what I did have was old castoffs and second- or third-hand items that I left for Jamie to keep or discard when she moved. The rest of my things had fit into the back of Jeff's Yukon in one trip.

When I brought the dress in, Jeff watched me hang it up in the closet, eyeing the white bag as if he could see through the opaque material.

"So it's done, huh?"

"Yeah. It didn't need much alteration, so it didn't take long."

Jeff leaned against the doorframe. "So I've been thinking more about our wedding. Since neither of us have much of anyone to come, except Jamie for you and Darren for me, we should just...be a little crazy."

He reached into his back pocket and pulled out an envelope and handed it to me. I opened it and pulled out two airline tickets to Las Vegas. I stared at the tickets, then back up to Jeff.

"I've got us booked to get married at the Venetian early next week." He grinned. "Jamie and Darren are both on board already. They've got rooms, flights, the works."

"Are you serious?" I examined the brochure. "You want to get married in Vegas?"

"I know it's not the traditional white chapel wedding with the works, but—"

"No, it's perfect. I've been trying to think about planning a real wedding, and my brain just freezes. This is...perfect."

"For real?" He let out a relieved breath. "I booked all this, deposits at the hotel and the tickets and the honeymoon and everything, but I wasn't sure if you'd be on board. I was kinda winging it and hoping."

"Where are we going on our honeymoon?"

He shook his head, grinning. "Nope. Not telling. It's a surprise."

I sidled over to him. "Sure you won't tell me?"

"No way. I've got everything arranged. Trust me."

I kissed his neck. "But I *really* want to know. Is it the Bahamas?"

He tilted his head back as I kissed his throat, unbuttoning his shirt and kissing my way downward. "Not telling. It's not the Bahamas, though."

I knelt in front of him and gazed up. "Sure there's nothing I can do to convince you to tell me?"

He laughed and tangled his fingers in my hair. "Not gonna work. I want it to be a surprise."

I unbuttoned his pants and pulled the zipper down. He was thickening in his underwear, bulging out against the cotton. "How about a hint?"

"You can do whatever you want, but I'm not telling. No hints."

I tugged his pants and boxers down, freeing his erection. "Hmm. Well, I'll have to try and change your mind."

His head thunked back against the doorframe as I licked his length from base to tip. "Anna, you're not gonna get anything out of me."

"Nothing?" I asked, sliding my palms around his girth.

"Well, nothing information-wise. Keeping doing that and you'll get *something* out of me, though."

I took him in my mouth, just the tip at first, my fist around his base and pumping slowly. "Hmmmmmm." I spat him out. "I can be very convincing."

He closed his eyes. "I know. But it won't work this time."

Still sliding my fist at his root, I moved my lips down his shaft. He groaned as I began to bob my head, working him with my hands in the same rhythm. Another groan, and his hips began to rock. When I could tell he was close, I slowed my hands to an imperceptible glide and took my mouth off him.

"God…damn. Not nice. Oh, god. I'm so close."

I laughed, and licked the tip of him in small circles. "How close are you?"

"So close. I'm gonna come…any second."

I stopped moving my hand. "So tell me." I wrapped my lips around the tip of him and sucked gently, not enough to bring him over the edge.

"You're impossible. Fine. We're going to an island."

I started pumping again and lifted my mouth enough to speak. "An island? The Caribbean?"

He hunched over, and I felt his cock throbbing in my hands, his fingers fisting in my hair. "I'm coming, Anna…"

I slowed. "Tell me!"

He huffed a laugh. "No! Not the Caribbean. Somewhere obscure. That's all I'll say. Now please…"

I felt his balls clench, and I nearly didn't get him in my mouth in time. He came as I was lowering my lips around him, and felt his seed hit my throat. I slid my hands on him, working his climax until he sagged against the frame.

He pulled me to my feet and held me against his chest, tilting my face to kiss me. "That was very underhanded of you," he said, a smile in his voice.

"Yes, it was. I told you I can be convincing."

He laughed. "But how much do you really know? An island that's not in the Caribbean. Doesn't really narrow it down much, does it?"

I frowned. "No, guess not." I shrugged. "But I really just wanted to see how much you'd tell me before you came. You can have your secrets. It'll be fun."

"You'd better start packing. Our flight leaves tomorrow afternoon."

"Tomorrow? I thought you said you had us booked for next week? It's only Thursday."

"Yeah, but we're gonna be in Vegas, baby! We can go the casinos and do touristy Vegas stuff, and then get married. An Army buddy of mine got married in Vegas, and he said it was a lot of fun. He gave me some tips."

I laughed. "How many 'Army buddies' do you have? It seems like I hear that phrase every single day, but I've never met any of them."

He chuckled. "Well, I use the phrase pretty loosely. Darren is my closest friend, he was my bunkmate in basic, and we were in the same unit all the way through every tour we did. He was one of the guys who pulled me out of the Humvee. He's the one with the property where I proposed to you. But I do have a lot of other guys that I know who are more acquaintances than real true friends, like people I see a lot or trust. We stay in touch, usually via email, and every few months we all get together on Darren's property and get wasted."

"And Darren is coming to Vegas."

"Yep. He's already got his ticket and a room on the same floor as Jamie."

"Is he single?" I asked.

Jeff frowned thoughtfully. "I think so. Why? You gonna try to hook them up?"

"Well, no. I was wondering if it would happen anyway, more than anything."

Jeff shrugged. "I don't know. It may, it may not. Darren is a good guy, but he's been through a lot, like me. He's hard to get close to."

I laughed. "You just described Jamie."

"Well, maybe they'd be good for each other."

"Maybe. I don't know. I made Jamie promise to stop having sex for a while."

Jeff chuckled. "And she actually agreed?"

"Says she promises."

"Why'd you do that?"

I shrugged. "Something just told me she needs to change her approach to things. She'll never find what she's looking for the way she's going about it."

Jeff kissed my cheekbone. "I agree. But until someone is ready to see things on their own, nothing you do or say, or even make them promise, will make any difference."

"I had to try," I said.

"I get it. You're a good friend." He turned me around and pushed me into the bedroom, smacking my ass. "Now get packing. I want to get to the airport early."

Chapter 6

WE SPENT THE FIRST FEW DAYS being tourists. It was a kind of combined bachelor/bachelorette party, as in Jeff, Darren, Jamie, and I spent much of those first two days in varying states of inebriation. None of us were big on actual gambling, so we spent a lot of the time exploring various attractions, playing slot machines with handfuls of quarters. I stood next to Jeff and cheered for him while he played blackjack, winning a couple thousand dollars before folding.

I could see Jeff being a top-notch poker player, since the entire time he was playing, at one point with almost three thousand dollars on the line, he never cracked a smile or broke a sweat. His face never changed expression. The only sign of stress was a slight narrowing of the eyes and thinning of the lips.

Jamie and Darren seemed to hit it off as friends, but I never saw any evidence of attraction beyond that. Maybe she was merely trying to keep her promise to me. Darren was the kind of guy she usually went for, tall, muscular, rugged, with pale blue eyes and buzzed blond hair. He and Jeff were cut from the same cloth, it seemed. Both were quiet men with slow tempers and deliberate gentility. There was a darkness to Darren that Jeff lacked, however, a sense of his personal demons lurking ever just beneath the surface.

Then, on Monday, the day before our wedding, Jeff told me he had somewhere he was taking me. He refused to say anything whatsoever about where or what, though, no matter how I pleaded with him.

I'm not very good with surprises, it seems.

I dressed in a button-down shirt and a knee-length skirt with bright purple tights, and he took me to dinner just off the Strip, and then had a cab bring us to a small casino. It was a little place, faded, a ways away from the bustle and brilliance of the main Strip.

"What are we doing here?" I asked.

"You'll see in just a second," Jeff said, leading me through the casino floor to the theater area.

Music pounded, muffled. I saw signs for a music festival of some sort, a list of band names, none of which I recognized as I scanned the list.

Jeff pulled me away from the sign and through a pair of doors. He already had tickets, and we were led into a concert area bustling with tattooed, pierced, spike-haired, ponytailed rock fans. The band on stage was loud, fast, and hard, rough vocals being growled into a mic by a thickset man with a braided beard down to his chest.

"Jeff, what is this?" I yelled into his ear.

He shook his head, pulling me with a firm grasp on my hand through the crowd until we were near the stage, off to the right and close to the edge of the crowd and only feet away from the VIP entrance.

The band on stage finished their song, played one more, a hard-driving instrumental number. When they exited, a metal song blared through the house speakers as the stage crew reset for the next band. In a surprisingly short time, the lights went down and the house speakers went quiet, and an MC brought a mic and stand out. A spotlight bathed the MC, who waited for the crowd to quiet.

"Our next band was a last-minute addition to the festival," the MC said. "I personally had a chance to see these guys play in New York a few months ago, and I was just blown away by their relentless energy and simply phenomenal talent. Please help me welcome, all the way from Detroit, Six Foot Tall!"

The MC swept an arm at the stage, on cue with the stage lights exploding to life. My heart stopped, my stomach clenched, and my blood went cold.

I turned in place to glare at Jeff. "What the fuck is this?"

"This is your last chance," he answered.

Further conversation was pointless. The drummer kicked a fast beat, and then they were off, a hard, driving number full of angst and anger. I couldn't make out much of the lyrics, but I had a feeling they were about me.

Chase was on fire. He wore nothing but leather pants and heavy black boots and thick, spiked leather cuffs on his forearms, spanning from wrist to elbow. He gripped an old-fashioned square handheld microphone in both hands and bounded from one side of the stage to the other, eyes blazing, thick muscles rippling on his bare, oiled torso.

I couldn't tear my eyes off him. I hadn't expected to ever see Chase again, yet here he was, in Las Vegas, the day before I was set to get married. Between numbers, I forced myself to turn and face Jeff.

"What is the meaning of this, Jeff Cartwright?"

Jeff's eyes were hard and serious. "I found out they were playing here the other day. I didn't plan this. But when I saw it was him, I had to know."

"Know what?"

Jeff pointed at the stage. "I'll never be him. I'll never be like him. I can't do that, I can't look like that. I can't be that. Can't, and won't." He reached into his back pocket and pulled out a VIP backstage pass on a lanyard. "I have to know if this is really what you want. If *I'm* really what you want."

"I chose you—" I started, but Jeff held up his hand, pushed the backstage pass into my hands.

"Like I said, last chance to get out. To get that," he said, with a gesture at the stage, and then he turned and made his way through the crowd, away from me.

I watched Jeff disappear, and then turned back to the stage. At that moment Chase was standing in the spotlight as the guitarist plucked a mournful intro melody. His eyes roved the crowd and found me. Shock rippled through him, so potent he almost dropped the mic. His gaze moved down to the VIP pass in my hands, and then I saw hope blossom on his face, quickly shut away.

Why would Jeff do this?

I couldn't figure it out. I thought I'd made my choice. I didn't think I'd ever have to feel Chase's eyes on me, waiting, ever again. But yet, there I was. I felt a presence beside me, smelled Jamie's familiar perfume. She didn't say anything; she only watched as Chase lifted the mic to his mouth, his eyes never leaving me. The look on Chase's face was haunting, full of longing. If I didn't know better, I might think all this had been scripted or arranged. The song was clearly about me, and now, by my sudden presence, sung directly to me.

"This next song is…special. It's brand new, you guys are the first live audience to hear it played. I wrote it during a time of…heartbreak and loss. Just listen, you'll see what I mean." Chase paused, and it was obvious he was struggling with emotion. "I hadn't planned this, but the person…the woman I wrote this song about, is in the audience today. Makes this performance especially personal. Anna, this is for you."

The guitar picked up volume and tempo; Chase closed his eyes, breathed deeply, then his eyes flicked open and focused on me.

He lifted the mic to his mouth and began to sing:

"I found you
floating between the pores of time
I found you
a dream of pale flesh and bright eyes
a fever dream
The moment our eyes met
I saw the gleam of need
and I couldn't resist
I found you
and I pulled you close
I found you
and I fell for you
but you walked away
I found myself
lost in the long dark night

watching the stars burn
watching your image fade
I found myself
dreaming in the dark
loving a ghost
a vision of you
not dead but gone all the same
I found myself
broken by you
blooded by you
I found you
a dream of pale flesh and bright eyes
a fever dream
I found you
nothing but a dream
I found you
nothing but a dream."

The song began as a haunting lullaby, sprightly and sweetly melodic, but always beneath there was a low, thrumming bass line weaving around the guitar chords and lyrics. When the words changed from "I found you" to "I found myself," the tempo picked up and the rhythm guitar started to chug, the bass began to pick up volume and discordant power, and the drums started to sprint, deep pounding bass drums and galloping snares. By the end of the song all was raging, the words no longer sung but screamed, and his eyes, god, his eyes, locked so laser-bright on me, until the crowd near me turned to see who he was singing to, screaming at with such pain and anger rife in his expression. He pointed, kneeling, when he began the last chorus, he pointed at me. The spotlights found me, frozen in place, eyes wide and terrified, heart pounding as loud as the bass drum.

Guitars went silent, drums faded, Chase's powerful voice quieted. All was motionless, a statue-still tableau, Chase's eyes fixed on mine. Jamie was next to me, her fingers gripping my arm in painful vise grip.

"*Do* something," Jamie hissed.

What could I do?

"You bastard." I wasn't sure if I meant Chase or Jeff.

I ripped the lanyard off my neck and shoved it at Jamie. The silence held, so profound that each shuffle of a foot, each clearing of a throat, was loud as a gunshot.

My words, spoken loud to carry to the stage, were audible to everyone. "I made my choice, Chase. I didn't want—I didn't come here on purpose. I'm sorry."

I turned and ran. The crowd parted for me. The double doors leading out to the casino floor stood in front of me, and I pushed them open.

Chase's voice froze me, raw and deep, amplified by the mammoth sound system. "Are you happy?"

I turned slowly and let the doors thump closed behind me. "What?"

"I asked if you're happy with him."

"Yes." I nodded, so that if he couldn't hear me clearly, he'd know my answer.

A charged pause sparked between us, even separated by hundreds of feet and hundreds of people. His eyes, his body, his presence, I couldn't help my physical response to him. I still wanted him, still desired him. My muscles trembled in memory of what he could do to me, of being tied up to his mercy. I pushed the traitorous image away. I didn't want that anymore. Not with him. I focused on Jeff's face, his hands, his body, his love. I felt the doors open, a brief cold breeze and a sense of openness behind me, and then Jeff's hard body brushed against my back. I leaned into him.

"Then that's all that matters," Chase said. His gaze flicked up to Jeff, and his next words were for him. "Take care of her."

I felt Jeff nod, once, curt.

Another pause, during which Chase turned away and addressed the band. There were nods all around, and then the drummer snapped his drum sticks together on a fast four-count. On the fourth clack of the sticks, the entire band burst into synchronized sound, the bass, rhythm guitar, and drums all matching with a driving heavy metal beat. Chase stood facing away from the crowd, mic held loosely by his side, bent at the waist and headbanging to the rhythm. I felt Jeff pulling me away, and I turned into him.

The song was brutal, hard-charging and pulsating with angst. I heard the opening lines growled with primal rage: "*How can I escape your eyes? I can't, I can't...How can I escape your lies? I can't, I can't—*"

Then the doors slid closed and the sound was muffled. I fell against Jeff's chest, sobbing.

"Why? Why did you do that to me?" I stepped back and slammed my fists into his broad chest. "I didn't *fucking* need that!"

"I'm sorry. But when I found out he was playing in Vegas, I just—"

"Had to test me?"

Jeff blew a long breath between pursed lips. "Yes, honestly. I also figured if he was here, and you were here, knowing your luck you'd run into him at the worst possible moment. Like, you'd be about to say 'I do' and he'd walk into the Venetian at that exact moment."

I tried to fight the laughter bubbling up at the image. "Yeah, that's exactly what would have happened."

"I'm sorry, Anna. I didn't mean to blindside you, but honestly, I had to know. I'm not Chase. I'm not some exciting, sexy rockstar. I like a quiet life."

"Why are you so hung up on this?" I asked him. "If I wanted someone like him, I would have chosen *him*. I chose *you*. I want *you*. Part of the reason I love you so much is that you're confident in who you are without being cocky. Why is it whenever he's around, or he comes up, you get all insecure?"

Jeff's eyes hardened. "Because you chose him over me once before, remember? Hard not to be insecure about that when I know you're capable of it."

My heart panged at the pain written in the lines of his face. "I guess I deserved that."

"Guess so." He looked away, and when he turned back to me, his eyes were softer. "Listen, Anna. I'm sorry. So sorry. I know that was really unfair of me to do. It wasn't about testing you—I mean, I guess it was, but...I can't lose you again. I can't. I saw the flyer for this music festival and I saw his band name on it, and I just...I froze."

I opened my mouth to say something, I wasn't even sure what, but he held up his hand to silence me.

"When you left me to go to New York, I knew—" His voice broke with a welter of potent emotion. "I knew what you were going for. You thought you might love him. Maybe you didn't think it in so many words, but I knew. I saw it. You thought you might love him more than you loved me. I...letting you go was the single hardest thing

I've ever done. I've buried buddies, Anna. I've buried best friends. But no lie, letting you go to him… that ripped me to shreds. You'll never know how hard that was—at least I hope you won't. I *cannot* go through that again. I watched you walk away, picking *him* over *me*. You went to New York and spent a week *fucking him*, when you'd just been with me. You know how hard that was for me? It was the longest week of my life. And then you came back, I knew you were back, I drove by your apartment and you were there, I saw you. I almost went up to the door, to talk to you, to—I don't know. Yell at you, or beg you to come to me. But I didn't. I waited. And you came back to me, wanting me because he'd hurt you. I wanted to kill him. No lie. But…you needed me. You need me."

Crowds flowed around us, oblivious, and music pounded on the other side of the door, Chase's band. Jeff paused, gathering himself.

"I need you, Anna. But if you want him, if there's any doubt in your mind that you might still care about him, then go. He's right through those doors, and he's still in love with you. He'll take you back. I had to know, Anna. I *had to*. I can't live through you picking him again. So if that's what you're gonna do, do it now." He held my face in his hands. "The last thing I ever wanted to do was cause you any more pain, and I'm so sorry. Forgive me for putting you through that. But I—I had to know."

I turned away from him to stare at the door, as if I could see Chase through it. I searched myself, scoured my heart and soul with brutal honesty; I owed Jeff that much.

I turned back to Jeff and let him see all of me in my eyes. "I choose you, Jeff. There's no doubt in my mind, no question. None. You are my heart and soul. He's my past. I'll never choose anyone but you for as long as I live. I wouldn't have agreed to marry you if that wasn't true." I let out a long breath. "Now, can we go? Or do you have any more *tests* for me?"

"Guess I deserved that," Jeff said.

"Guess so."

He took my face in his hands and kissed me. I resisted, turned away from his kiss for the one and only time in our romantic relationship. I was still angry at him for bludgeoning me with Chase.

"No." I ripped free from his arms. "I'm mad at you."

I walked out of the casino and hailed a cab, Jeff trailing behind me. I climbed into the cab and gave the driver our hotel name. Jeff sat in silence beside me, picking at his fingernails.

My lips tingled from the force of Jeff's kiss. It had been furious, demanding kiss, claiming me as his. My anger was fading, but I refused to give in to Jeff just yet. I could tell he felt bad, but I wasn't ready to let him off the hook yet. I hadn't deserved to be blindsided like that, not with Chase, not when I'd already endured the agony of having to choose. I didn't love Chase, but he hadn't deserved that shock, either, especially not during a public performance. The pain in his eyes had nearly broken my heart all over again.

I knew why Jeff had done it, though, and I didn't blame him, not now that my anger was receding. I *had* chosen Chase over Jeff once upon a time, and even though a deep, dark, secret place inside me held on to the memories of my time with Chase, I did regret having left Jeff. I regretted having hurt him, having broken his trust in me.

I couldn't change that, but I could prove to Jeff I only wanted him. I decided to prove it the only way I knew how.

We got back to our hotel room, and I waited behind Jeff while he slid the card into the lock reader. Seconds seemed to stretch out, the light turning green with a soft *click*, the door sliding open on oiled hinges, my heart thudding in my chest as if we were going into the room to make love for the first time, rather than the thousandth time. My hands shook, a cold sweat broke out on the small of my back, and a burning flush of desire flamed my cheeks, turned my panties damp.

A few short steps through, and then the door latched closed behind me. Jeff released my hand and kept walking, settling on the edge of the bed and leaning his elbows on his knees and his face in his hands.

I pressed my back to the door, watching him. He remained there, breathing, upset. I smiled, but he didn't see it. I plucked open a button of my shirt, and then another, and then the shirt was open and I dropped it on the floor at my feet. He didn't hear the rustle of fabric or the soft *plop* of cotton hitting the floor. I slid my feet out of my flats, unrolled my knee-high purple stockings, slowly unzipped the side of my skirt. He heard the zipper then. His eyes narrowed in confusion, and he straightened on the bed.

My bra joined the pile of clothing on the floor, followed by my panties, and then I was naked, too-cold hotel room air pebbling my skin and making my nipples harden. I swayed toward Jeff, and he crawled backward on to the bed. He sat up to take me in his hands, but I pushed him down with a hand on his chest. I peeled his shirt over his head, straddling his khaki-clad hips, leaning forward to draw the T-shirt off, my breasts swaying over his face. He nipped a breast with sharp, gentle teeth, but I refused to gasp. I slid down his body, unbuttoned his pants, and pulled them off.

His cock was rigid, lying flat against his belly, rising and falling with his short, panting breaths. I teased him with my fingers, touching his pur-ple-veined length with my fingertips, tracing the groove beneath the head with my tongue. I wrapped both palms around his cock and took his tight sack in my mouth, gently sucking it between my lips, one side and then the other. He gasped, arched his back, groaned my name as I caressed his shaft and suckled his balls.

I waited until he was moments from coming into my hands, and then I released him and crawled up his body, rising up on my knees above him, palms braced flat on the wall, my slit poised above his mouth.

"Make me come, Jeff," I said, my voice hoarse, low and rough.

"Yes, my love."

He suited action to words and slid his palms up my thighs to the cleft of my pussy, slipping a single long middle finger into my wet folds, using his other hand to pull me down to his mouth. His tongue found my clit and swiped slow circles around it, each touch of his tongue a line of fire, burning pleasure into my heat-slick blossom.

I forced myself to stay still as his finger moved within me and his tongue speared against my clit. I arched my back and allowed myself a single soft whimper as waves of ecstasy rose through me. A hand cupped my breast, testing its weight, and then pinched my nipple at the same time as his tongue punched against my aching, sensitive nub.

He pulled his finger out, added his index finger, and slipped them back in, but this time his pinky finger was extended, and it bumped gently and insistently against the rosebud knot of muscle.

He paused, asking silent permission.

"Do it," I said.

His smallest finger kneaded the muscle, relaxing it, and then his fingers were gone briefly, replaced by wet warmth slicking the tighter entrance. He slipped his pinky into me at the same time that his tongue found my clit and his first and middle fingers found my pussy, and then I was writhing helplessly above him, explosions rocking through me, drilling sensation to the wildest heights of furious orgasm, wringing me into a gasping, begging puddle on top of him, his fingers gone, my ass on his chest, my body curled over and sliding downward, downward, pierced slowly and subtly by his thick, hot shaft. No chance of recovery for me, only pleasure so potent it became pain, too much to bear, but instead of begging him to stop, I heard my voice whispering ragged pleas in his ear:

"Jeff, my love, please don't stop, don't stop..." even though I couldn't take any more of him, couldn't come any harder without ripping in half, without bursting into helpless sobs.

He didn't relent, but drove into me with his characteristic slow, powerful strokes, pushing deeper and deeper.

I rolled off him without warning, as he was about to come. I heard his teeth grinding as he struggled to hold it back, and then he lifted up on an elbow and watched me settle on my knees and forearms, presenting myself to him, my face turned to the side, a seductive smile on my lips inviting him wordlessly.

Like a lion he prowled on his hands and knees behind me, his cock slipping between the globes of my ass. His nails raked painfully, sweetly down my back, gripped my hips, and then, with a single tilt of his pelvis, he was inside my pussy and driving, god, so deep. I bit the blanket to stifle a scream, climaxing a third time on the instant of penetration.

It didn't take him long to find his release. He thrust, thrust, thrust, and then a deep, rumbling growl announced his climax. He drove into me, hard, bowling me forward, his hands pulling me back, and then again, a primal plunge of his cock, fingers digging into my hipbones and clawing me back into him.

Even blanket-muffled, my scream of delight was loud in the still, cold air. His roar of release was louder.

We lay side by side, and I nuzzled my head onto his shoulder.

"I love *you*, Jeff. Only you. Forever." I tangled my fingers with his, my left hand in his right, dim light glinting dully off the facets of my engagement ring.

"Damn right, only me forever," he said, a smile in his voice.

"Cocky bastard," I laughed.

"It's why you love me."

"One of the many reasons."

He tilted my chin up with an index finger and kissed me, long and slow and drowning with passion. "I love you, Anna Devine," he said when our lips parted.

"After tomorrow I'll be Anna Cartwright," I pointed out.

"I like the sound of that."

"Me too." We drowsed in the dreaming dark, until a thought struck me. "You know, we never wrote our vows."

"Huh. You're right," Jeff mused. After a moment, he said, "Well, I've got an idea for mine. Just write yours from the heart. Doesn't have to be complicated. Tell me you'll love me forever and always, no matter what."

"I can do that."

"I know you can." He pulled me closer. "Now go to sleep. We've got a busy day tomorrow."

Chapter 7

I woke to my nose being tickled. I swatted at the offending sensation, encountering small, soft hands. I forced my eyes open to see Jamie sitting next to me on the bed, cross-legged, dressed in a tiny skirt and tight T-shirt. She had a tendril of her copper hair in her fingers and was brushing my nose with it.

"Wake up, sleepy-head," she said in a sing-song voice.

"Unh-uh. Go away." I slapped at her half-heartedly.

I knew her better than to think she'd leave me alone. She scrambled off the bed and pulled the covers off me. I curled in a ball, moaning in protest as the cold air hit my naked body.

"God, woman, you stink of sex. Get up and take a shower."

I rolled up to a sitting position and rubbed my eyes. "Where's Jeff?"

She waved her hand. "Oh, off with Darren. Picking up his tux and getting ready. Whatever guys do before weddings."

"What are we doing?" I caught the robe Jamie handed me and wrapped it around me.

"First, coffee. Second, a shower. Third, breakfast." She brought me a cup of Caribou coffee, because she knows I hate Starbucks' over-roasted coffee, even though I love their espresso drinks.

I sipped slowly as I stood up and went to the window to peer out the curtain. It was another glorious Las Vegas day.

I'm getting married today. It didn't seem real. Was it really going to happen? An actual wedding? Jeff had sprung this whole thing on me, and I had no idea what was going on. Panic hit me, and I focused on breathing through the hammering of my heart, sipping my coffee.

Jamie slid her arm around my waist and rested her head on my shoulder. "Hey, it's going to be great, you know. I can feel you panicking. Don't."

"Easy for you to say. I have no idea what's going on. Did he actually plan this thing, or is he just winging it?"

Jamie laughed. "He has this thing planned down to every little detail. You'll be shocked. I'm, like, mega-impressed. If I believed in romance, or weddings, I'd say this was the most romantic wedding ever." She sighed. "I believe in this wedding. I'm not going to ruin any of the surprises, but you should relax, because he's got it all covered. He loves you."

"I know he does. I should know better than to think Jeff would leave this to the last minute, because he never leaves anything to the last minute. But…it's a Vegas wedding. I'm worried it's going to be something from a bad romantic comedy. Like, the minister will be this fat old Elvis impersonator, and we'll be driven away in a pink Cadillac with tin cans hanging off the back and it'll be the most embarrassing day of my life."

"You're ridiculous. Do you really think Jeff is that stupid or tasteless?"

I shook my head. "No, but that's what my fears are telling me will happen."

Jamie rolled her eyes. "Well, that's not what's happening, so quit freaking yourself out. I told you, he's *got* this."

I finished my coffee, and Jamie followed me into the bathroom, sitting on the closed toilet while I showered.

"You know, when I first heard your wedding was in Vegas, I kinda had similar expectations,"

Jamie said. "Some tiny little chapel way off the Strip, bad piano music, and yes, an Elvis impersonator for the minister. But Jeff showed me some of what he had planned, and I'm telling you, it's going to be amazing. You'll love it."

"What happens after breakfast? Which is what, bagels and cream cheese?"

"Breakfast is whatever you want. Order in, go out, whatever. We have some time. After that, we have part one of wedding day surprises. So get your ass moving."

"I thought you said we had time."

"Yeah, but not all day. 'Sides, I'm hungry."

Breakfast was omelets and toast at a nearby diner, and then Jamie hailed a cab and gave the driver a slip of paper with our destination written on it. We ended up at a spa a few minutes' drive away from the main downtown area.

"Come on, " Jamie said, climbing out. "This is part one. The full treatment at a day spa."

"Serious?"

Jamie grinned. "You and me, baby. Get ready for some serious pampering."

My throat closed up, and my eyes burned. I blinked away tears and followed Jamie inside. Jeff really had planned everything out, and the fact that he'd included Jamie in the day spa treatment made me choke up even worse.

I made it through the manicure before the question that had been tickling the back of my mind popped out. "So, Jay. What happened after I left the concert?"

Her long hesitation piqued my curiosity, and my worry.

"Um. Nothing?"

"Jay."

"Fine. I went backstage and hung out with the band. We partied. Darren showed up at some point, and things got crazy." She pretended not to notice my suspicious glare.

I picked up a cotton ball from the counter nearby and threw it at her. "Jamie. Talk. You're not telling me something."

"Ugh. Why does it matter?"

"Because you'd tell me if it didn't matter," I said.

"Hooker," she muttered. "Fine. Like I said, we partied. There were lots of people, girls were all over the guys from the band. Chase was all angsty and broody. Darren and I sort of hit it off, stuck together since we knew each other better than anyone else that was there. It was all groupies except for Darren and me."

"Darren is totally your type. Jeff says he's single."

"Yeah, but remember that promise you made me make?"

I lifted an eyebrow at her. "Break it already?"

"No." When my eyebrow lifted even higher, she protested loudly, "I didn't! I promise."

"Then what?"

"Nothing happened. I just...that song Chase sang to you? That whole thing was *hot*. I know he was hurt and you were hurt and it was all hurty. But...god, I can see why you were hung up on him. He's—"

"Fucking amazing. I know. Please don't remind me. I'm getting married today, remember? To Jeff. Chase is old news. History. He means nothing to me anymore."

I watched Jamie as she fidgeted in her seat.

"I know. I just feel bad for him, is all. He's stuck on you."

"This is a weird conversation," I said. "By way of changing the topic...so you and Darren?"

She shook her head slowly. "No, I don't think so. The vow of celibacy thing has its merits, I have to admit. Once upon a time, I would have fucked that boy silly. I still want to. But our conversation about empty sex keeps running through my head, and I just can't...I don't know. Darren is nice. He's hot, he's totally my type, you're right about that. But I can't see anything working with him long term. I don't know why. It just wouldn't work. I think he's...what is it? He's dark. I've done the dark and angry guy long enough. If I'm going to break this

vow of celibacy, I want it to be with someone...
different from what I usually go for. Someone better. Someone who could give me what you have
with Jeff." She paused for a long moment. "I'm
jealous, you know. Of you and Jeff. I've never told
you that, but I'm finally able to admit it. I'm green
with envy. You're so happy, and he's doing all this
for you..."

"You'll find it, Jay. You will."

She was silent then, and I could sense there was
something else she wasn't saying, but the prickles
were out, and I didn't push it.

After the pedicures and facials and waxing,
Jamie seemed to have pushed away whatever was
eating at her. During the massage, Jamie blurted a
question that floored me.

"Are you and Jeff going to have kids?"

"What?" I saw double for a second. "Kids?
God, Jamie. I haven't even gotten married yet. I
don't know. It's never come up."

"Well, can you see yourself with a kid?"

I thought about it. "Um. I guess? It's never
crossed my mind. I honestly don't know."

"If you happened to get pregnant, like whoops.
How would you feel?"

"God, Jamie, what's with the cracked-out questions? Are you pregnant or something?"

"Me? Hell, no!"

"Then what is this?" I groaned as the masseuse hit a knot and bore down on it.

"I don't know. You getting married and this whole vow of celibacy thing has really messed with my head."

I tried to picture myself as a mother and failed completely. "I don't know, Jamie. I don't know a damn thing about kids. I have no nieces or nephews, no friends with kids. If I got pregnant, I would be scared, I think. But...excited, too, probably, once I got over the whole shitting-myself-with-terror part. Do I really have to think about this? I'm panicking enough as it is without you jinxing me with a sudden pregnancy or something."

"Sorry, sorry. I don't know what's gotten into me. My brains been going a mile a minute for days now."

I laughed. "Maybe the constant sex was dulling your brain. Now that you're not in a constant state of sexual arousal, maybe you'll think more clearly."

Jamie snorted. "You couldn't be more wrong, girlfriend. I'm hornier than ever! Not having had sex in so long—"

"It's been less than a week."

She continued as if I hadn't interrupted. "—has turned me into a raging fucking horndog. I'm honestly worried I'll end up jump the first thing with a cock at some point." She shuddered. "I haven't even gotten myself off, Anna. It's awful. I can't stop thinking about sex. I feel like a guy. I should scratch my vag every time I think about sex and rename myself James. It's that bad. Like, all the time."

"Right now?"

"God, yes. Like, even talking to you, I'm thinking I could just roll over and whip this towel off and me and masseuse boy here can go at it on the massage table."

The masseuse, Todd, a toned young blond man with a carefully sculpted goatee, laughed. "Sorry, sweetheart. Wrong team. And we're not that kind of establishment anyway."

"Damn it," she laughed. "Just as well, I guess. It wouldn't be good to break my vow this quick."

Todd made an odd face. "You really took a vow of celibacy? Like no sex? At *all*?"

Jamie sighed theatrically. "Yes. No sex. At all. It's all her fault. She thinks it'll help me find the man of my dreams or some shit."

He bobbled his head back and forth. "Hmmm. Interesting idea. Is it working?"

"Not so far. But like she said, it's only been a week. If it works, I have a feeling it'll take longer than a week."

"Well, good luck," he said. "I can't imagine what that must be like. I'm already boy-crazy as it is. If I had to go a week without so much as a blow job I think I'd actually die."

Jamie giggled. "Yeah. Exactly how I feel."

"But you—" He cut himself off with a laugh, slapping her shoulder playfully. "Oh. You dirty little slut!"

"Thus the vow of celibacy," Jamie said. Then she craned her neck to look at the masseuse. "Are you allowed to call your clients names?"

He quirked an eyebrow. "You're buck-ass naked, honey. I can say whatever I want."

"Oh. Well." Jamie frowned. "I never thought about it that way."

"Most people don't," he said.

"Honestly, though," Jamie said, "it really does change the way you think, I'm discovering. Especially if you're boy-crazy like me. I've always had someone around. I got to rely on them for my self-esteem, in a way. Like, they make me feel sexy, and they want me, so it gives me a power over them. But that's different than feeling it from inside myself, you know? Not looking at every hot guy and wondering how fast I can get his pants off is actually kind of liberating."

"Really?" Todd asked.

"No kidding. If I can make this stick for a while, it might be a really good thing."

"Hmmm," Todd said. "I think my boyfriend is about to break up with me. Maybe I'll give it a shot. I think I'll set a goal, like two weeks at first, and see where it goes from there."

"I should get a medal if I make it two weeks," Jamie said.

I looked at her. She was acting nonchalant, but something in her voice had me thinking she had someone in mind who was threatening her vow. She met my eyes, and something passed between us, a kind of unspoken agreement. I wouldn't ask, and when she was ready, she'd tell me.

The next surprise of the day was an appointment at a high-end salon, where my hair and makeup were done with artistic care. Jamie was quiet for much of it, but with enough judicious use of outright mockery, I got her back into sassy form. After my hair and makeup were done, we went back to the hotel to finally get me into my dress.

"Jamie, you have to help me write my vows."

She looked at me as if I'd grown horns. "Two things. One: you haven't written them yet? And two: me? Are you crazy?"

I snorted. "No, I haven't. I've been sort of busy, if you hadn't noticed. But fine, I'll write them myself. Just give me some time alone before we put me in my dress."

"I think it's time for another cup of coffee. I'll be back later." She left the room with an airy wave.

I stared at the pad of hotel stationery, with absolutely no clue what to write. And then Jeff's advice floated into my mind: *Just write them from the heart. Tell him I love him forever and always.*

My pen scratched along the paper, the words flowing easily once I got started. The paper had a few wet blotches by the time I was done.

Jamie came back with a cup of coffee for me, and we drank together in peaceful silence. I let Jamie read my vows.

She handed the paper back with a sniff. "Damn it, girl. You've made me cry. We don't cry. And we just had our makeup done."

I handed her a Kleenex. "We do now."

"When did that happen?"

I shrugged. "I don't know. But I'm learning to be okay with it. Crying doesn't have to be a sign of weakness. It just means we're human. We're women, and we have emotions."

"Gah. Whatever." She rubbed at her eyes in irritation. "I still hate crying, even if you *are* right. Now, get your sexy ass up, and let's put on a wedding dress."

I focused on breathing. Breathe in, clutch the bouquet of roses in trembling fingers; breathe out, one slow step forward. Wide double doors were pulled open from within the chapel, revealing a dozen dark wood pews, each pew garlanded at the aisle-end with a bow of white silk and a single pink rose. The aisle itself was covered in pale pink rose petals.

My heart was beating so hard I thought the entire chapel could hear it pounding like a drum.

When the doors opened, an older woman with sil-ver hair began Mendelssohn's "Wedding March" on a grand piano. I was shaking so bad the roses trembled in my hands. My knees were weak, my throat thick and burning.

A male voice cleared his throat from beside me, a deliberate *ahem* to catch my attention. I turned and nearly fainted. Jared stood next to me in his full dress uniform. He looked so different, so much older. I hadn't seen him in so long…. He had new lines around his eyes, a leaner, rangier build. His eyes were like mine, hazel and expressive, and his hair was the color mine would be, chocolate brown. He gave me a bolstering smile and held his arm out for me, and I had to choke back a sob.

"Jared? When did you get here? And how?" I whispered, looking up at him.

He bumped me with his shoulder. "Jeff knew someone who got me some emergency leave," he whispered back. "Pulled some strings, called me, and here I am. Just got in an hour ago. Your boy up there is a keeper, sis."

"Yeah," I said. "That's why I'm in this dress."

He laughed. "Yeah. Now quit talking to me and look at your husband," Jared said. "I think he's trying to catch your eyes."

I'd been avoiding looking at Jeff because I was worried it would make me burst into hysterics. I was near to hyperventilating as it was, and with

Jared's unexpected presence to walk me down the aisle, I was even closer to the edge of breakdown. I tore my gaze away from my brother and met Jeff's eyes. A single tear dripped down my cheek, and I wiped it away.

He was resplendent in a traditional tuxedo, his eyes wavering with emotion as he watched me. As if sensing my nerves, he smiled at me and mouthed *I love you*. My nerves receded, my tears evaporated, and I could move again. I'd been rooted to the spot at the doors, Jamie behind me holding my train. Now, with his eyes on me, loving me, I was able to take the first step forward.

The aisle wasn't all that long, but the measured walk from the doors to *him* seemed to take an eternity. With each step, I realized more fully how ready I was for this. I didn't think I would be, even when I agreed to marry him. I worried, all the way up until the moment I saw him at the altar, that I wouldn't be ready. But I was.

I'm ready. I want to do this.

With every step closer to the man I loved, I realized that this was exactly what I wanted, and you couldn't have dragged me away from the altar with a thousand wild horses.

At long last I reached him. A step up, a second, and then his hands were in mine, holding me, steadying me. His eyes burned into mine, the love in his gaze bringing tears of happiness to my eyes. I didn't wipe them away.

"Dearly beloved," the minister began, "we are gathered here today to celebrate the blessed union of this man and this woman…"

It really sank in then, as the minister began his brief sermon:

I'm getting married.

There was no "dearly beloved" besides Darren, Jamie, and Jared. But then I peeked out at the chapel and saw a man a few years older than Jeff who I took to be his brother sitting next to an older woman with graying hair and eyes dark brown like Jeff's.

I took a deep, wavering breath to steady myself, clutching Jeff's hands for dear life. I tuned in to the minister's words of advice regarding marriage, trite platitudes that suddenly took on new meaning as I contemplated the reality of being married to Jeff. Then came the vows. The minister turned to me first, and Jamie reached up to hand me my sheet of paper.

I needed several breaths to calm myself enough to speak. "Jeff, I wish I could explain to you how much you mean to me. I wish I had words to say how deeply entwined you are into the woman I've become. You've swept me off my feet and turned my life into a fairytale, because you are my happily ever after. I don't care what's happened in the past, and I'm not worried about what will happen in the future. All I need is you with me, every day. Most wedding vows have promises like 'in sickness and in health, for richer or for poorer.' I promise you those things. Of course I do. Money, health, those things are a part of life. What I promise you is forever. I promise you all of me. I promise you every last shred of myself, day in, day out, no matter what. Even when you're being a stupid jerk." I laughed, half-sobbing, and took a moment to compose myself.

"I'm never a stupid jerk," Jeff said.

I wiped my cheeks. "Yes, you are. Now shut up and let me say my vows. I'm not done." I scanned the paper and found my spot, near the end. "I promise to love you, even when I don't feel like it. I promise to take care of you. I promise to listen to you, because you're usually right. I promise, above everything, to be faithful to you, and *only you*, for as long as we both live. I love you, Jeff Cartwright."

The minister nodded and turned to Jeff. "And your vows?"

Jeff grinned. "Mine are a bit...different. Darren?"

Darren reached into his suit coat pocket and pulled out a wireless microphone, handed it to Jeff. Music began to play from the PA system, soft country strains. I recognized the song: "Wanted" by Hunter Hayes.

Jeff lifted the mic to his lips, and for the second time in two days, a man sang to me. This time was different. If I hadn't already known it, Jeff singing a sweet country song to me as his vows proved I'd made the right choice. I didn't feel on the spot, or pressured, or frightened. This was a soft serenade, a dedication set to music.

His arm went around my waist, my hand joined his on the mic and I sang the harmony, our bodies swaying to the rhythm, our eyes locked on each other. Everything faded except the music, except Jeff's deep, strong voice weaving around mine, the words of the song with their soul-deep, so-perfect meaning.

I didn't need the words of the song to hear Jeff's promises to me. They were written in his eyes. They were proven in the way he loved me, in the fact of this wedding. I would be wanted, every day. I would be loved, every moment.

The song ended, but Jeff stood holding me, one arm around my waist, one hand on the mic. "I know you heard what I was saying with that song," Jeff said, "but it's just not enough. Forever isn't enough. No words are enough. But yeah. I want to make you feel wanted every minute of your life. I want to wrap you up and protect you. I want you to know how completely I cherish you, I want you to know it when you wake up, and when you fall asleep. I want to make the things that hurt you not hurt so bad. I want my love to fill you when you're empty, and make you overflow when you're full. I want every moment of our life together to be your fairytale, your happily ever after. I'm no knight in shining armor, no prince charming, but I'll sure as hell try, every single day."

He paused, thinking. "Remember what I said to you, not too long ago?"

Somehow I did know exactly what he was going to say, and I said it with him. "The time I've spent with you is better than anything I've ever known."

He laughed, brushing my face with his rough palm. "Yeah, of course you remember. Well, that'll be true for always, every day until the day we die. I love you, Anna."

The minister waited until he was sure we were both done speaking. "Anna, repeat after me."

"I, Anna, take you, Jeff..."

I repeated the words, and my voice broke on "I do." I'd held it together up till then, but at those two words, I fell apart. Jeff's thumb swept my tears away, and his palm cupped my cheeks as he repeated the same words. His voice went low and rough at the "I do," his hand around the mic, still held between us, trembling.

"I now pronounce you man and wife. You may kiss the bride."

My arms went around him, my fingers curling in the hair at the base of his neck, our lips meeting, our bodies crushing together. I lost myself in that kiss, drowned in the revelry of belonging. He was mine, and I was his.

Cheering erupted from the entrance to the chapel, too many voices raised and hands clapping to be just the three people in attendance. We broke the kiss and turned to look: a crowd had gathered at the doors to the chapel, drawn from the hotel by the sound of our singing, our amplified vows. We laughed together, and I wiped my eyes on the shoulder of Jeff's tuxedo coat.

My throat caught again as I scanned the chapel. I saw Darren, Jamie, and Jared, and there at the back, nearly hidden in the crowd of onlookers, was my mother. I looked to Jeff.

He shrugged, shaking his head. "I didn't know for sure if she'd be here. I called and invited her, but...I wasn't sure she'd come. I hope it's okay."

"I'm glad she's here." I stared up into his rich brown eyes. "Thank you for this. All of this. Thank you, so much."

He kissed me lightly. "I wanted to give you a wedding you'd remember. I know this wasn't a traditional thing, but—"

I shut him up with a kiss. "This was perfect. Absolutely perfect. It's exactly what I wanted. I can't believe you got Jared here to give me away!"

He turned with me, and we moved down the aisle toward the doors. "It was tricky, but I knew a guy who has an uncle in the Corps. You needed someone to give you away."

We made it to the end of the aisle. I felt Jamie fiddling with my train behind me, but I only had eyes for Mom. Suddenly I couldn't remember why I hadn't seen in her in so long; I knew I'd remember as soon as we tried to have a real conversation, but in that moment it didn't matter. She'd shown up for my wedding, and to the part of me that was still a little girl wanting her mother's approval, it was enough.

"Hi, Mom."

"Hi, sweetheart," she said, kissing me on both cheeks, European-style. "I'd say thank you for inviting me, but you seem surprised to see me."

"Well, it's a bit of a surprise wedding. I'm glad you're here, though."

Mom laughed. "What's a surprise wedding? You didn't plan this?"

I shrugged. "Not really. I mean, I knew I was getting married, but Jeff surprised me with pretty much everything else."

"Wow. Quite a surprise, then," she said, with a wry arch of her eyebrow.

Jeff seemed to sense my discomfort with the direction the conversation was taking. "I'm glad you could make it, Laura. I know it means a lot to Anna for you to be here. We'll see you at the reception. Jamie will make sure you know where you're going."

He pulled me into a walk, and I squeezed his arm gratefully.

When we were out of earshot, I leaned up to whisper into his ear. "See what I mean?"

He chuckled. "Yeah, subtle digs. I can see how that would wear on a person."

I rolled my eyes. "Oh, you have no idea. She was just warming up. And she's more forthright than Ed. Eventually she'll just come out and say what she's thinking. Ed won't. He'll just keep digging, keep poking." I craned my head to search the crowd. "I don't see Ed, speaking of whom."

"Guess he couldn't make it."

"Guess not," I said. "Fine with me. Now, where's the reception?"

"Oh, I reserved a private room downstairs. Cake, catering, that kinda stuff. Nothing fancy. Just an excuse to eat and get tipsy before we go on our honeymoon."

"Speaking of our honeymoon—"

"Nope. Still not telling." He glanced at me and grinned. "You're more than welcome to try and… convince me again, though."

I laughed. "Hmmm. Not a bad idea. Although I have something a bit more…involved in mind.

And I'm not sure I can get on my knees in this dress anyway."

We were moving through the crowd of onlookers, who were enthusiastically calling out encouragement and congratulations. Apparently someone heard my comment about not being able to get on my knees, and I heard several bawdy suggestions to give it a try. Jeff and I laughed them off and made our way to the private room where the reception would be held.

It was one of the smaller conference rooms of the hotel, but something told me even a relatively small room like this wouldn't be cheap to rent out, even for an hour or two.

"Jeff, how'd you afford all this?" I asked.

He winked at me. "A man's gotta have his secrets, doesn't he?"

"Not from his wife, he doesn't."

He laughed. "I had a bit of money saved. I put it to good use. And that's all you'll get out of me."

"But all of this had to have cost—"

He spun me to face him. "It doesn't matter. It was worth it. You're worth it. It's just money."

"But, Jeff—"

He kissed me silent. "Honey. Let's not have this conversation now. Just relax and let me take care of you. Please?"

I relented with a sigh. "Fine. But only because you look so hot in your tux."

He ran his hands over my hips, pulled me flush against him. "You know, Jamie was right about the dress. I did almost faint when I saw you. All the blood rushed south."

I ground my hips against his, feeling the evidence of his arousal. "Wish we could sneak away somewhere and...take care of your...problem down there."

He chuckled. "I'm not sure that's physically possible in a wedding dress. All that tulle seems like it'd get in the way."

I laughed. "I don't think it's tulle, actually. But you're probably right. We'll just have to wait."

It was a long wait. The food was good, the drinks were plentiful, and the music loud. We were only half a dozen people, but we had fun. Jeff had even arranged for a small cake, two tiers, red velvet with thick buttercream frosting.

After a couple of hours, Jamie announced, in her brash style, that the party was over and we were leaving for the airport. I hugged Mom, said goodbye, and promised to call her when we got back. I spent the longest goodbye with Jared.

"I wish we had more time together," I said, hugging him.

He squeezed me tight, spoke into my hair. "I know. Me, too. But we'll see each other again soon. I've got a longer leave coming up over the holidays. I'll spend it with you and Jeff."

Jamie came next. "Have fun, Anna. Make sure you get up off your back at least once during the honeymoon, huh?"

I snorted. "Honey, real women do it on top. You should know that."

"Well, then, at least let him up every once in a while. Go swimming or something."

"Yeah, I'll give him breaks to eat. But not many."

She shook her head. "You're making me horny. Go. Get out of here."

I pinned her with a glare. "Remember your vow. Make it worth it."

"Don't remind me," she said. I lifted an eyebrow. "I will. I *will*. I promise. Quit worrying about me. You have a plane to catch, Anna. Get going."

Jeff had a limo waiting for us. We changed in our hotel room, leaving my dress and Jeff's tux for Jamie and Darren to take care of. We climbed into the limo and were soon speeding out of downtown Las Vegas for the airport.

Once we were underway, Jeff turned on some music, locked the privacy window, and then turned to me. "You were saying about later?"

The heat in his gaze sent quivers of desire fluttering through me. He'd put on a tight T-shirt, and his muscles strained against the thin cotton as he reached for me. We were sitting on opposite benches of the limo, our knees brushing. I felt

an electric tingle shoot through me where his leg
nudged mine, his touch as thrilling now as the first
time I'd made love to him, in his shower at his
house.

I had a flash of that encounter, his tanned skin
and broad muscles sluicing with hot water, steam
wreathing around him, his eyes wary and full of
desire. He reached for me now as he had then, with
gentle and implacable strength. He pulled me to sit
on his lap, but I moved out of his reach, kneeling
in front of him on the floor.

I'd changed into a calf-length skirt and T-shirt.
I lifted my skirt slowly up past my thighs, swaying to the music. Inch by inch I showed Jeff—*my
husband*, I thought, tasting the phrase—my bare
thighs, my bare hips, my bare pussy. I stretched
back in the seat, spreading my thighs as Jeff crawled
across the limo to kneel between my legs. He ran
his fingers up my calves to my thighs, parted my
folds to press his mouth my cleft. He lifted my legs
onto his shoulders, and I pulled him closer to me,
tangling my fingers in his hair.

His tongue speared into me, and I let him lap
at me a moment or two and then pulled him up
to kiss him, fumbling with his belt, button, and
zipper. He sprang free, and I pushed him to a sitting position and sat astride him. I lifted myself up
and poised there, one hand braced on the roof, the
other grasping Jeff's thick shaft.

I pushed his tip into my folds, nudged my clit with the broad head, and moved him in circles against my stiffened nub, eliciting small gasps from me. Jeff slid his palms up my belly and my sides, pulled the cups of my bra down to free my breasts. His fingers pinched my nipples, rolled them, and then his soft lips found my skin, and he kissed his way over the mounded flesh to graze his teeth over my nipples. My thighs trembled with the effort of holding myself up at an awkward angle, and with desire. I moved his cock in quickening circles around my clit until my knees were buckling with the rhythm, and when I could bear it no longer, I sank down on him, impaling him deep inside me. We gasped in tandem, a Muse song drowning our voices.

I felt the limo slow and move through a series of turns, telling me we were moving through the airport.

"I think we're almost there," I said, rising and sinking on his shaft slowly.

"Not yet," Jeff said. "I'm not there yet."

I giggled. "No, I meant at the airport."

"Oh." Jeff pulled my head down for a kiss. "Well, that's awkward. I'm not done with you yet."

I leaned onto him, my arms around his neck, looking down into his molten chocolate eyes. He thrust up into me, slow, deliberate strokes. He reached over with one hand and hit the intercom.

"Give us a few minutes before you drop us off, please, driver."

"Yes, sir."

I thought I detected a faint trace of amusement in the driver's voice, but then Jeff's pistoning hips took on an increased urgency, and I lost all capacity for thought. I pressed my face into his neck and rolled my hips, keeping my weight on my shins to allow Jeff room to move. His hands slid down my hips to cup my ass and lift me up, then let me lower down onto him, driving him deep.

Climax washed through me, slow, powerful waves sweeping me away. I heard my voice whispering Jeff's name into the sweat-salted skin of his neck. His teeth nipped my earlobe, his hands on my ass moving me faster and faster now, and the rolling wave of orgasm crashed over me, so intense I could only cling limp to Jeff as he pushed, pushed, pushed into me, gritting his teeth to keep from roaring aloud as he came with a series of savagely powerful thrusts.

We shuddered together through the aftershocks, and then Jeff rolled in place to set me down and pulled out of me. He rummaged in a console, found a box of Kleenex, and used them to clean us both.

"You can drop us off, driver," Jeff said into the intercom.

"Very good, sir."

I pulled my skirt down and smoothed the wrinkles out, then stuffed my breasts back into my bra.

"You may want to, ah, fix your hair," Jeff said.

I rummaged through my purse and found a compact. "Oh, god. I have just-fucked hair." I pushed and pulled at the loose curls for a few seconds, then gave it up as a lost cause and pulled it back into a ponytail.

"Hey," Jeff said, "I happen to like the just-fucked look on you."

"Yeah, I bet you do," I said, grinning at him. "You give it to me often enough."

"I don't hear you complaining."

"Hell, no," I said. "You can give me just-fucked hair whenever you want."

"I'll hold you to that," Jeff said, pinching my ass as I moved toward the door.

The driver opened the door and we slid out, our bags waiting for us on the sidewalk. Jeff tipped the driver, and we moved through the crowd, Jeff in front, leading me by the hand. We checked our suitcases, and Jeff pulled me through the bustling airport to international departures, and from there to a gate buzzing with waiting travelers.

"Wait a second," I said, after scanning the departures screen. "You said we were going to an island. This says Paris."

Jeff smirked. "Surprise?"

I smacked his arm. "You lied to me!"

He laughed. "I didn't lie. It was...deliberate misinformation." He leaned close and whispered in my ear. "Besides, you had my cock in your mouth. I told you what you wanted to hear so you'd keep doing it."

"You're a sneaky bastard," I said.

"Yeah, well, you didn't think I'd actually tell you what I was planning, did you?"

I frowned. "Yeah, I kind of did."

He kissed me, laughing still. "Well, obviously it didn't work. You can try again later, though. Maybe I'll give up some of my other surprises, if you're...persuasive enough."

My arms slid around his waist. "Other surprises?"

"Yep. You never know what I might have planned."

"We're going to Paris. What else could you possibly have planned?"

He shrugged. "Like I said. You never know. You'll just have to wait and find out. Or you can try and...coerce it out of me."

I snorted. "You're really pleased with yourself about that, aren't you?"

"Yeah, a little. You really did almost get it out of me, though. A little more teasing, and you might have gotten the truth."

"So I just have to tease you long enough?"

"Shit."

I slid my hands into his back pockets. "I'll have to remember that." I kissed his mouth next to his lips. "So, why Paris?"

He bobbed his head side to side. "Well, it was just an idea that hit me. Remember when we sang that Faith Hill and Tim McGraw song together, for that couple's anniversary?"

I smiled at the memory. "Yeah, I love that song. The video is *so* awesome."

"That video is why I picked Paris. That song makes me think of us and of Paris, so it seemed like it might be a fun place to spend our honeymoon."

The boarding call echoed over the speakers, and we joined the crowd lining up.

"It's perfect," I said. "You and me in Paris, just like Faith and Tim."

"Exactly," Jeff said, smiling.

Chapter 8

PARIS WAS EVERYTHING I'd ever thought it would be. Winding streets, narrow alleys, quaint cafés, and expensive shops. It was beautiful and cultured and haughty. We spent the first few days too busy exploring the city to do much more at night besides fall asleep in our huge hotel bed. The third day we agreed to separate in a department store and buy something for the other, something reasonably priced and fun.

I bought lingerie, something sultry and lacy that I'd never wear except to turn Jeff on, the kind of thing I didn't expect to have actually stay on my body for long. It was a pair of black and red lace panties, cut high in front, and a bustier to match, strapless, pushing up my breasts to overflowing, cupping my every curve, displaying my body. The clerk wrapped my purchase in a plain brown paper bag, and I carried it with me to meet Jeff for dinner at Cafe Flo on the top floor of The Printemps department store. Words failed me as I walked in. The ceiling was stained glass, an impossible dome of a million, million colors, panes of hand-painted glass rising in an infinite jigsaw puzzle of pastels. The stained glass descended on all sides to maybe a dozen feet above my head as I stood staring up, neck craned to gawk at the elegant ceiling.

I wasn't the only one gawking. An older man bumped into me as he stared up, excusing himself in German. I saw Jeff leaning on a wall, watching me, a small opaque plastic bag in his hand, a store logo printed in French on the side. As I didn't speak or read French, I had no idea what kind of store he'd gone to.

I crossed the café and pressed myself against him, meeting his lips with mine. "What'd you buy me?" I asked.

Jeff grinned mischievously. "You'll have to wait and find out." He reached for my bag. "What about you?"

I held it out of reach, laughing. "I don't think so! You'll have to wait, too, buster. Unless you want to show me yours, in which I'll show you mine."

"I'm kidding," Jeff said, taking my free hand. "Let's eat, I'm hungry."

We ate at a mirrored table, which provided a view of the magnificent ceiling even as we dined. We talked about the various sights we'd seen, and would like to see. We finished eating and strolled slowly through the dark Parisian night back to our hotel. We stood in our room, the blinds open to let in the glittering topaz lights of the city and the lit spire of the Eiffel Tower in the distance. For a long moment neither of us spoke, just looked at each other, the room unlit, shadows long and our hearts beating in unison.

I tore myself away from his gaze and took myself into the bathroom to change into my new lingerie. Nerves pulsed like fire in my blood as I stripped naked, rinsed off in the shower, primped my hair and redid my makeup, spritzed perfume on myself, and then pulled the negligible bits of lace from the bag.

This was new for me. I'd been in my bra and panties in front of Jeff on any number of occasions. I was comfortable in my skin with him; he thought I was beautiful and spared no effort to make sure I knew he thought so. But to wrap myself in lace for him, to present myself to him as a gift...this was different. I slipped the panties on, fitted myself into the bustier, and plumped my breasts before looking at myself in the mirror.

When I did, I stopped breathing for a moment. I saw myself, yet again, as Jeff might see me. And then, with a shock, I realized I wasn't merely see-ing myself through *his* eyes, I was seeing myself through my own eyes. It was a strange, almost diz-zying, metaphysical understanding. I was finally learning to see myself as beautiful. Not simply because Jeff thought so, but through his endless repetitions, through his demonstration, through constant love and reassurance.

My hair floated loose in golden waves around my shoulders, framing my hazel eyes and high cheekbones. My bare shoulders were delicate, my breasts lifted high and full, spilling out for his hands to touch. My sides were held in to accentu-ate the swell of my hips and my lace-clad buttocks. My legs were long and bare, smooth and pale as porcelain.

I was a sensual, sexual woman, and in this lin-gerie I was a vision of tantalizing eroticism. My nerves faded into nothing, replaced by a river of heat in my belly. Jeff was waiting just beyond the door, and I knew how his eyes would widen when he saw me, how his hands would curl at his sides as if grasping my flesh, how his cock would tighten inside his pants.

I let out a deep breath and twisted the knob, pushed open the door, and stepped through to stand a foot away from Jeff. He had sat down on the edge of the bed, his shoes kicked off, and was rolling and unrolling the paper bag holding his gift to me. When he saw me, his eyes went wide and his jaw went slack.

A confident smile crept across my face at the stunned awe on his face.

"God*damn*, Anna. You look—just...damn." He stood up and took a hesitant step toward me. "Are you really meant for me? This isn't a dream?"

I laughed and stepped closer; mere inches separated us, but he hadn't touched me yet.

"Yes, my love. I'm all yours." I swept my hands down my curves. "This is your gift. Do you like it?"

"Do I like it? My god, Anna. I've never seen anything as beautiful in all my life as you right now."

"Then unwrap me."

"Not yet. First I want to just look at you." He gently pushed me toward the bed.

He opened the paper bag and withdrew two sets of fuzzy purple handcuffs and a matching purple velvet blindfold.

"You bought handcuffs and a blindfold?" I asked.

"Yeah, well, no. I mean, I bought them in Vegas and brought them here. This isn't what I bought you at the store," he said, toying with the blindfold. "I don't know how you feel about this kind of stuff, but I thought it might be fun. Exciting. You know? What do you think?"

"Jeff, I don't want you to think we need this stuff to be exciting."

"No," he said. "I don't. But I mean, do you want to?"

I smiled at him, a small seductive curl of my lips. "Slap those cuffs on me, bad boy."

Jeff licked his lips, then approached me with the first set of cuffs. I stretched my right wrist over to the bedpost, and Jeff gently curled the bracelet around my wrist and clicked it in place.

"Is it too tight?" he asked.

I shook my head. "No, it's fine." He hooked the other side of the cuff to the bedpost, then did my left wrist. "You can do anything you want to me, now. I'm at your mercy."

He stood staring at me for so long I started to squirm under his gaze. Eventually, he reached for the hem of his shirt and peeled it off, then slipped out of his pants so he stood naked in front of me. His cock stood straining straight up, thick and purple-veined, hard and begging to be touched. I lay, cuffed to the bed, wanting desperately to touch him, to take him into my mouth, to feel him slide between my lips and my palms and the folds of my pussy.

"Jeff...let me touch you," I said. "Come here so I can taste you. Let me put your big cock in my mouth."

Jeff gaze went heavy and hooded. "Uh-uh. No. I wouldn't last three seconds if you did that. Just looking at you like that, cuffed and helpless, wet and ready for me...I'm so hard I'm about to come without even touching you."

"What are you gonna do?" I asked.

He grinned and stepped toward the bed, his cock bobbing as he moved. He took the blindfold and wrapped it around his eyes, tied it in back, and crawled onto the bed near my feet. He took my foot in one hand, slid his palm up my shin to my knee, traced the circumference of my thigh from one side to the other. His finger trailed up my other leg, tickling gently along the inside to the lace "V" of my panties. I writhed my hips into his fingers, feeling dampness moisten the black fabric as he barely brushed up the mound of my pussy to the band of my panties.

"Oh, Jeff...I love the way you touch me. Take them off, please."

He smiled beneath the blindfold. "Not yet, sweetness." He ran a finger underneath the waistband, teasing me. "I'm not ready for you naked yet. I'll get there, though."

He lowered his face to my leg, kissing up my thigh from knee to my hipbone.

"You take everything so slow," I said. "Have I ever told you how much I love that about you?"

He paused with his lips on my belly and turned his face to me. "You do?"

"Yes," I said, sucking in my belly in anticipation as he resumed kissing my flesh ever farther downward, now at the inside of my thighs. "It's so delicious. It—oh, god, yes, right there—makes everything...just better."

"You like it slow, huh?" A hint of something in his voice made me shiver. "Well, then, I'm gonna have to go *real* slow, aren't I?"

He pressed his mouth to my pussy through the lace and breathed on me, a long, slow, hot breath. I moaned and writhed on the bed, wanting his fingers in me, or his tongue on me, or something, but he refused to even slip a single finger under the elastic to touch my bare flesh.

Instead, he traced a fingernail over my pussy where his breath had blown, the lace and the flesh beneath still hot. I trembled and thrust with my hips, but he drew away and laved his tongue along the inside of my thigh parallel to the elastic band.

"God, Jeff, touch me, please!"

He only laughed, another blast of heat on my folds. "Already begging, my love? This is gonna be so much fun." He bit the soft skin of my thigh, hard enough to draw a yelp of protest. "You're handcuffed, Anna. Did you think I wasn't going to draw this out as long as I could? I have you helpless. I could draw this out for hours. I could feed you, and give you water, and never ever let you come. You're so expressive. I know exactly when you're getting close to coming."

Something like real fear shot through me; he was perfectly capable of torturing me with near-orgasm, I realized. "You wouldn't."

He tugged the waist of the panties down to the very edge of the crease of my nether lips and dipped his tongue in, a mere brush against the sensitive skin, but it was enough to make me cry out.

"Oh, no? You don't think I would?" His voice dared me to think otherwise.

"Please, Jeff..."

"Please what?" His tongue dipped back into the crease and slid toward my clit.

"Please, touch me. Let me feel you. I want you inside me."

"Oh...no. I don't think so. Not yet. You aren't screaming my name yet, baby. You're not even really begging me properly yet."

What have I done?

I'd known he would tease me, but he seemed to be dead set on truly teasing me into hysteria.

Jeff pulled the panties lower, exposing my clit, giving me hope. My body was on fire, every nerve ending alive with hope of stimulation. He hadn't touched me above my waistline.

My breath huffed in and out, and I made my first pull against the handcuffs. He laughed and speared his tongue against my clit, giving me my first taste of near-climax. He left the panties where they were and removed his mouth from my skin, exploring me now with his fingertips. He drifted from kneecap to inner thigh, traced up the line of my pussy, brushing briefly over my clit and across my hips, the merest grazing of the pads of his fingers, crawling slowly over my flesh. His fingers slid up under the edge of the bustier, touching my ribs and the padding of flesh over them, just beneath the wire of the bra.

Touch me! I pleaded silently, but the words wouldn't come out past my panting breath. He clawed his nails slowly and gently down my sides, gathering inward toward my wet, aching folds. My hips involuntarily left the bed as he drew closer, closer, nearing the goal, across the smooth-waxed mound and—

Down either thigh, drawing a desperate whimper from my lips. I wanted him to touch me, *needed* to feel his fingers dip inside me. I knew he wouldn't give me his cock, not yet, but surely he would slide a finger into me, give me a taste of release?

He curled his fingers into the panties at my hips and drew them down farther.

"Yes, yes...please," I whispered.

He kissed my belly, my side, my hipbone, the edge of my pelvis above the lace panties, and then... yes, he licked my clit, a single slow swipe of his hot, wet tongue, and then a second, even slower. While his tongue made its aching path against my clit, his fingers danced up my thighs and hooked inside my panties, brushing my cleft, and my entire body lifted off the bed, bridging with shoulders and feet. He lapped against me yet again, and now hope blossomed through me, tangled with the rising phoenix of orgasm.

Abruptly his tongue and fingers were gone, and he was kissing my shoulder, his weight hovering over me but not touching, a felt presence. I lifted my head to watch him, felt a thrill of excitement at the sight of his naked body over mine, covering me, his broad shoulder and back rippling with heavy slabs of muscle, the burn scars ridged ropes glinting in the moonlight and city light. His buttocks flashed pale and hard as he stretched over me, his palms planted on either side of my breasts, his arms tree-thick and his cock throbbing against my belly.

I felt an upwelling of love, a roaring inferno of passion for this man, even as he tortured me with sweet, ecstatic pleasure. His lips moved against my clavicle, touched my throat, gentle as a thought, slid stuttering slickly down my breastbone to kiss the heaped flesh of one breast, the right, and then the other. His cock bobbed against my belly, so close but so far; I strained downward against the handcuffs, seeking to get him inside me. He moved with me, though, kissing my breast inch by inch, only the exposed flesh. I waited for him to pull the cup down and begin the slow tease of my nipple.

After an agony of minutes spent kissing my breasts as if he'd never touched them before, never tasted them before, he finally tugged one cup down enough to let a nipple pop free. He kissed his way toward it, and I found myself holding my breath as he circled the hard-standing bead of nerves with his tongue.

He teased it with gentle nips of his teeth, light flicks of his tongue, moist pinches with his lips, and then, without warning, he bit the nipple hard enough to make me buck up off the bed with a squeal.

"Too hard?" Even teasing he couldn't help worrying about hurting me.

I shook my head, then realized he couldn't see me. "No," I gasped, "just...shocked me. Any harder would be too hard."

He didn't answer, went back to flicking my nipple with his tongue, licking in a rhythm that set my hips undulating. His fingers met my clit on my hips' up thrust, and I gasped at the sudden pressure, sudden burst of intense pleasure. As quick as the full thrust of his fingers against me appeared, it vanished again just as fast.

"No, Jeff, please, bring it back..."

For once he did as I asked, sliding his fingers along my belly to cup my pussy, a molasses-slow molding against my folds. His middle finger moved inexorably inward, slipping under the panties to dive inside me, the first full penetration.

I moaned, a long, throaty voicing of relief. He added his ring finger, and then moved them together deeper inside me until his pinky and index finger were splayed on either side of my labia. He swiped in, curled in, brushed the rough patch of my G-spot, and this time I shrieked aloud.

My hips were writhing as alive, bucking and gyrating, a silent plea to keep stroking me, keep going, don't stop. His fingers moved inside me, pushing the waves of climax higher and higher, until the waves were on the verge of breaking within me.

"Are you about to come, baby?" Jeff's voice spoke from between my legs, his breath huffing on my thigh. "Are you so close?"

I knew, even in my desperation, if I told him I was mere moments from coming, he'd stop.

"No?" My voice was a breathy squeak, and my hips gave the lie.

His fingers went still inside me, but didn't withdraw. "Oh, I think you are. I can hear it in your voice. Your pussy is so tight around my fingers, and the way you move against me? Yeah, you're close. I bet if I licked your clit, just once, you'd come so *fucking* hard, wouldn't you, baby?"

I couldn't help the answer ripping from my lips. "Yes! Please, give it to me, Jeff."

His tongue swiped next to my labia, one side and then other, stroked in beneath my clit, licked just above it. I undulated against him, dying to feel the wet heat of his tongue against my clit, desperate for climax.

The waves of orgasm floated away, lessened and shrank, and then, right then, he flicked the button of my clit with his tongue, just once, bringing me back the edge. But then his mouth swept upward along my belly to kiss my cheekbone, my forehead, my chin, my lips, exploring my face as his hands skimmed over my skin, over the lace of the bustier beneath my breasts.

He pushed his hands beneath my back, and I lifted up to let him touch me, anywhere and everywhere. He followed the line of clasps along my spine, exploring the catches. I rolled to my side, my arms twisted unnaturally. He unhooked the uppermost clasp, then the next, and his lips pressed burning kisses to my skin where it was exposed by the widening gap between the edges of the bustier. With each released eyelet, my breasts gained weight.

With each kiss to my skin, the velvet blindfold brushed my skin, soft and cold against the heat of my skin. I'd forgotten for a moment he was doing all this by touch alone. He knew my body so intimately, was so familiar with my every curve that he could explore me blindfolded, kiss my face and unerringly find my breast from mere memory. I imagined I was him for a moment, smelling the scent of my soap and the light dusting of perfume, silky skin beneath his lips, flesh firm in his hands.

The way he worshipped me told me I was beautiful. The loving and delicate way he kissed my flesh told me how desperately he desired me. The slight tremble of hands on my back as he released the final clasp to free my breasts told me how much he wanted to forget the game and ravage me hard and fast with primal fury. The fact that he continued to move with aching, tender slowness told me he cherished each salty touch of skin to his lips, each gasp elicited from my lips.

He hadn't said the words "I love you" since he handcuffed me to the bed and began his blind mapping of my body. He didn't need to; the feather-soft grazing of his fingers across my skin spoke the words for him, the gentle crush of his lips to my breast made the words clear to me, the effortless strength with which he lifted my body to strip off my panties showed me how much he loved me.

I stopped fighting, stopped wishing for climax, and closed my eyes, lay back in the bed and let him love me, as slow as he wanted. This wasn't about any kind of chemical orgasm any longer. This was pure adoration made physical. I was finally naked beneath him, my bare breasts cupped in his hands and lifted to his lips to kiss and taste and touch, my nipples sucked into his mouth and drawn taut, bringing fire rushing to my loins and bursting through me, a shuddering precursor of the earth-quake to come.

He slid up my skin, the soft, leaking head of his cock stuttering along the inside of my thigh, bump-ing against my entrance. I held my breath, straining helplessly against the bonds restraining me from touching him. I wanted to hold him, needing to feel his firm flesh under my hands, but I couldn't. All I could do was lie tensed and coiled for the moment of his body's slide into mine. I drew my knees up, and my shoulders lifted off the bed as I sought to curl closer around him.

His lips caressed my breast, first the right, then the left, brushing underneath each one, carving around the sides, coming to a stop on my nipple. All the while his hands were cupping my hips and dipping between my thighs to tease me with a quick finger slipping in between my slick lips before retreating and tricking my clit with a circling tip. I gasped and whimpered, sounds brought forth from me without volition, my entire body now writhing against him, begging him to move inside me.

"Jeff, please, I'm begging you, please let me feel you inside me. I need it. I want it so bad. I need your cock inside me. Please!"

He sucked my lip into his mouth, silencing me, stroking my pussy with his fingers, drawing me toward the cliff of orgasm. His thick, hard cock was probing my entrance just beneath his hands, and now he braced himself above me, his broad, essence-slick head touching my clit, sending me into paroxysms of need.

"Beg me again, baby," Jeff whispered.

I wrapped my legs around him, struggled to pull him closer, but he resisted me, held himself in place. "Please, Jeff! Give it to me. I want to feel you inside me."

"Tell me more. Tell me exactly what you want," he said. "I love hearing you talk dirty to me."

"Yeah? You want me to tell you how bad I want your cock?" I gave myself over to his game. "I want it, baby. I want your cock. I need you to slip it into my pussy. I don't care if you go slow or fast, I just need to feel your big, hard cock fill me."

Jeff moaned, a low growl against my skin. He pulsed his hips, pushing his cock against my clit, and I gasped in pleasure as an electric thrill zapped through me. He did it again, and I crushed my pussy against him, moving with furious desperation.

"You want it inside you?" he asked. "Right now?"

"Yes! Please, yes!"

He kissed me, thrusting his tongue into my mouth at the same time as he drove his cock into me. "Like that?"

I let myself scream out loud. "Yes! Oh, god, Jeff, thank you...god!"

He buried himself to the hilt and held there, filling me but not moving. His teeth grazed my nipple, and I knew if he had thrust as he bit me I would have come, but he didn't. He held himself motionless, deep inside me. This was a new kind of torture. I was filled by him, but if he didn't move I wouldn't find the release I needed. He spent sweet, slow moments kissing my breasts, toying with my nipples, licking them in a quick rhythm to mock the motion I wanted his hips to make.

His body covered mine, his weight pressed down on me in the intimate crush of hard male angles on soft female curves. I moved, wiggled, writhed, not just for the glide in and slip out but to feel his skin against mine, to feel his knees inside my thighs, his chest against my breasts, his belly flat against mine. I moved against him only to feel the merge of flesh with flesh, the flutter of hearts beating in sync, the sinfully sweet slip of skin slick with sweat, sliding silk in the searing susurrus of sex. The words naming this union ceased to matter. This was sex, this was love, this was primal fuck-ing and intimate lovemaking, this was the baring of self to self, mind to mind, heart to heart.

I heard no sound but his breathing, each inbreath my name whispered on his quivering lips. He moved then, as he spoke my name.

"Anna," and his manhood slid out of my sex, paused at the slick opening, his lips met mine in a soft, sugar-sweet kiss, and he moved into me, slower than the glacial slide of ice down mountains.

I didn't dare breathe, didn't dare so much as flutter an eyelid, held still so the only motion was the beating of my heart and the pumping of blood in my veins. Statue-still, stone-still. His shaft pushing into my desire-damp blossom was the slowest pulsing of a drifting wind, a gliding of silk on skin, a gradual infilling of my body with his. I gasped as he pushed into me, wept his name as he slid back out, whimpered in delight with the feel of his thickness slicking into my heat.

I jerked against the chains, tears dripping down my cheeks, seeking to curl closer, cling tighter, keep him in me, pull him faster. He kept the slowest motion possible, sliding into me like mercury merging, splitting apart and rejoining. He moved with the speed of continents spreading apart, a dozen heartbeats passing between the time of his tip drifting in and his hips bumping mine. I continued to weep, unabashed, feeling climax rise in me, a flood of release pooling like an ocean of potential energy poised on the brink of flash flooding into kinetic rush.

He didn't stop, now. He moved, slid, slipped. He kissed my tears and whispered my name, held my curves close, poured his love into me without words. My feet hooked around his waist, held him inside me. I clamped down with my inner muscles, desperate to keep him deep. He groaned when my vaginal walls clutched his cock, holding him tight.

Move and breathe, pulse and pull. The push and pull of lungs filling and releasing, the pump of our hearts spreading lifeblood, these mirrored the sliding of his body into mine, the perfect merge of body into body.

Time slowed, stopped. His face buried into my neck, my breasts crushed up into his chest and my hips crashed against his and we came, we came, bursting together like a storm breaking on the shore, like waves splashing on the sand.

I shattered beneath him, broke apart under his body. I felt him fill me, each thrust of his cock into my throbbing channel like heartbeat, felt the jet of wet heat hit my walls, and then he thrust again and the wash of seed spread through me again, and my inner muscles clenched his shaft, lights bursting behind my tight-closed eyes, fire blossoming in my every fiber. I couldn't breathe for the detonation of my body, couldn't help but scream and weep and call his name, gasp his name, plead his name. Still he moved, slow and deliberate. His pace never changed, even as he came, even when I climaxed underneath him.

His hands cupped my face and we kissed, trembling lips on lips, love passing between like shared breath. I felt him push the blindfold down at last to dangle from his neck, and our eyes met, sparks flying, tears sliding down faces. He wept, too, and I kissed his cheeks, tasted salt.

He snatched the key from the bedside table and unlocked my wrists, the cuffs dangling free. I snaked my arms around his neck and crushed my mouth to his, freedom lending me renewed passion.

Time faded as we lay side by side, breathing, kissing, holding each other. I felt his manhood stir and gathered him in my hands, caressed him into hardness, sat astride him. He reached up and closed a cuff around his wrist, and I did the same to the other side, and then we were bound together, fingers tangled, hands sliding along bodies. My fingers traced my hips as he touched me. Together we grasped his shaft and guided him into me, and then he lay back and I supported my weight on his hands, fingers twined, my hips undulating on him. He stared up at me, the purple blindfold a swath of darkness against his tanned skin.

Motion became liquid, no longer in and out or up and down but wave crashing into wave. I gave into desperation, collapsed on top of him and rode him like a runaway stallion, fast and furious, my hair draped around my face and sticking to my sweat-damp cheeks and forehead, plunging my love-mad hips on his as hard as possible, crashing with bruising force.

Orgasm was a nuclear explosion mushrooming within us in tandem. I felt him splash his seed into me as I burst above him, around him. Again and again we came together. I felt him come, but his cock throbbed hard inside me and I continued to move on him, riding him, and then I felt him impossibly hard and huge and coming again.

Mouth pressed to mouth, quivering wide in silent screams, we came together, merging and morphing until I had no conception of myself without him.

His dark brown eyes glittered in the silver light of the fading moon, piercing mine, and finally he spoke the words aloud: "I love you, Anna."

"I love you more," I said.

He laughed, and rolled me onto my back and kissed me with the fire of a thousand suns.

We slept, and woke, and made love with starving hunger, and slept again. At some point the blindfold went around my eyes and I made love to Jeff in perfect dark, feeling only his body on mine, smelling the scent of sex and sweat and Jeff.

At some point day came and went, and only the hunger in our bellies told us of the passage of time.

When we slept again, it was the sleep of utter exhaustion and completely satiety.

We woke and showered and dressed, found a cafe and had a late lunch.

"The clerk at the front desk told me about this bridge that's somewhere around here," Jeff said around a bite of brie cheese. "Apparently you buy a padlock and write your names on it, both you and your lover, and then you lock it on the bridge and it will seal your love for as long as the lock remains on the bridge."

He pulled a small heart-shaped padlock out of his pocket, along with a Sharpie. "I got this as your gift. I thought it would be fun to do. I guess there's these bridges with love locks on them all over the world, in cities in Belgium and Japan and a bunch of other places."

He wrote his name on one side of the lock and handed it to me, and I wrote mine. For the first time, I signed my name *Anna Cartwright*. I smiled as I showed it to him.

"Anna Cartwright," Jeff said, leaning over the table to kiss me. "My wife."

"I like the way that sounds," I said.

"Me, too."

We took the lock to the *Pont de l'Archevêché*, opened the lock, hooked in an open spot, and clicked it into place.

"You know there are two such bridges as this?" a voice said in a thick French accent. An older man, with silver hair and a carefully trimmed beard, shuffled over to us. "You look as if you are in love, yes? Not only lovers, but in love?"

"We just got married a few days ago," I answered.

"Ah, well, *mademoiselle*, then you are in the wrong place, I think. This, the *Pont de l'Archevêché*, it is for lovers, you know? You have the key, still?" I showed him the key in my hand, and he took it from me, unlocked our lock, and handed it to me. "You must take this to the *Pont des Arts* and place there your lock. When you have locked it, you must throw the key into the Seine. There you are claiming the tradition of the committed lover, *oui*? It is a different kind of love, not only for the sex, but for the staying together, the always love. *Oui*?"

Jeff and I exchanged amused glances. "Thanks," Jeff said. "Wouldn't want to invoke the wrong tradition."

The old man narrowed his eyes. "You make fun, but this is serious. What can it hurt to believe? You should have more faith, non?"

"I wasn't—" Jeff started, but I stepped on his foot, and he smiled at the man. "Thanks, for real. Um, how do we get there?"

The old man gave us directions, and we found the bridge after a few wrong turns. The railings of this bridge had far fewer locks. Jeff and I put our padlock in place and withdrew the key. Before we tossed it into the Seine, Jeff pulled me against his chest and kissed me, hard and full of passion.

"I don't know if this how this works," he said. "But I think we should make a wish before we throw this key in."

I laughed. "I'm pretty sure that's how this works, but I'm game."

He wrapped his huge hand around my smaller one, holding the key together. "I wish for forty years of marriage with you," he said.

"Only forty?" I teased.

"Fine. How old are we? Almost thirty for both of us? How about eighty years, then? We'll be over a hundred. If we're still alive in eighty years, I want to still be married to you. Still in love. Still kissing you, just like this—" and he caressed my lips with his, slow and delicate, then hungrily, "every single day, until we fall asleep together and wake up in heaven."

"To kiss you every single day already is heaven," I whispered, "And that's my wish. A million kisses, and then a million more."

We threw the key into the Seine. It made a tiny splash, but I knew, deep in my soul, that the image of the key hitting the rushing river would be ingrained in my mind for as long as I lived. The feel of Jeff's hand in mine, a gentle breeze ruffling our hair, evening in Paris lowering gloom around us, these would be memories locked in my mind forever.

The End

Here's a Sneak Peek at

Rock Stars Do It Harder

Part One of Chase's Story
Coming Soon

THE PAIN IN ANNA'S EYES when she caught sight of Chase sent a bolt of agony through his heart. It was the ultimate rejection, even more than her words. She'd told him, in no uncertain terms, that she didn't love him. Even that didn't hurt quite so much as seeing her soft, sweet, expressive hazel eyes blaze with pain and surprise and anger at the mere sight of him.

Chase had thrown himself into the band, into tours and concerts. He wrote like a madman, pouring his pain and anger into songs that got progressively darker as the weeks passed. His band mates had noticed, but they didn't say anything. The darker music drew the fans, drew the crowds to swelling numbers, filled the stadiums and the bars and the casinos. Sure, they weren't headliners yet, but of all the opening acts, Six Foot Tall drew the most attention, garnered the loudest applause.

None of that mattered. Not to Chase.

The fans could scream their heads off, but it wouldn't fill the ache in Chase's heart, the hollow in his belly. Only *she* could fill him like that, and she'd chosen someone else. Even when fans sneaked backstage after shows and pressed their bodies against him, he couldn't find even a moment of contentment.

He'd let a girl take him all the way once— and only once—after Anna broke his heart. He'd rejected dozens of girls up until then, all skinny girls with small, hard breasts and waists he could span with his hands, ribs showing when they lifted their tops to tempt him with their pale, frail bodies. He'd rejected them all, politely but firmly.

Then a different kind of girl found him backstage, bribed security to give her a few minutes alone with Chase. She was tall with wide hips and heavy breasts, a luxurious fall of black hair and bright green eyes. For the first time in weeks, Chase felt the stirrings of desire. He let her peel her shirt off, pendulous breasts swaying in front of his face, her aureolas dark dimes against her pale skin. She'd pushed her skintight pants down to her feet and stepped out to stand before him naked and gloriously beautiful, a pale Diana. The cold air of the dressing room made her nipples stand on end, hard little beads.

Chase sat, waiting, heart thudding, his pose deceptively casual. She didn't say anything, just unbuckled his belt, tugged his pants down to his knees, slipped her legs astride his, and impaled herself on him, moved above him, her green eyes locked on his, full lips pressed thin, heavy breasts swaying. His body responded, but his mind stayed frozen and cold, his heart empty and black.

She isn't Anna. He pounded the thought through his mind, a harsh reminder, but to no avail. Black hair flashed into blond locks, green eyes turned gray. Her name was poised on his lips, whispered in the cold air.

Her nostrils flared and her eyes narrowed, the black-haired beauty, but she smiled and said, "I can be your Anna, if that's what you want."

She moved faster above him, her eyes closed, and her breath came faster as she neared climax.

He came, and the release was brief and unfulfilling. She rose off him, plucked a few Kleenex from the box on the counter behind Chase. He watched with a kind of detached, apathetic disgust as she cleaned the white trickle from her thighs, swiped down the line of her lips, and then threw the tissue in the small metal trashcan on the floor. She dressed, pulled her long black hair into a ponytail, and opened the door. Before she departed, she pulled a small white rectangle from her purse, a business card, and set it on the filing cabinet by the door.

"If you get over Anna and you want some real company, call me." Then she was gone.

Chase sat, his pants still around his thighs, cock limp and sticky against his leg. A fist knocked, jerking Chase from his blank stare, and he tugged his pants on, buckled his belt, and called a hoarse, "Come in."

The security guard poked his head in. "You're on in five." He saw the card on the cabinet, and flicked a grin at Chase. "Nice, huh? That chick had some big ol' titties, right?"

"Yeah."

"Gonna bring her backstage again after?"

"No." Chase felt a flood of self-loathing wash through him. "In fact, don't let anyone else back here again."

The security guard lifted an eyebrow in surprise. "You sure? You don't want—"

"No, I don't."

"All right, man. If you say so."

After that Chase had taken to hiding in the green room, or in a crowd of other musicians. He'd started to heal, started to forget.

And then he'd gone out onstage in Vegas, some casino way off the Strip. The lights had gone up, the crowd had been wild, manic, infusing him with a crazed energy. The first number had killed. Then he'd paused, scanning the crowd, seeing only a sea of faces. Just as Chase was about to give the signal to kick in the next number, he'd seen a flash of blonde hair, an all-too-familiar face only a few feet away from the stage.

Anna.

One look, and his heart had crumbled all over again.

He'd written dozens of songs about her, but he'd only written one song *to* her, *for* her. It was, perhaps, his best song to date. The band had learned it, but they hadn't planned on performing it yet.

It was time, he decided.

Chase spun in place and waved for his band's attention. "We're doing 'I Found You.'"

"Now?" This was Gage, his bassist, and one of his oldest friends.

"Yeah, now. She's here. She needs to hear it."

Gage shrugged. "If you say so, man."

"Make it burn, boys," Chase said. He turned away and fixed his eyes on Anna.

Mic to his lips, he addressed her. "This next song is...special. It's brand new, you guys are the first live audience to hear it played. I wrote it during a time of...heartbreak and loss. Just listen, you'll see what I mean." Chase paused to tamp down the emotion. "I hadn't planned this, but the person... the woman I wrote this song about, is in the audience today. Makes this performance especially personal. Anna, this is for you."

He watched her eyes darken with pain, and then the drumbeat kicked in and the music carried him away. He screamed himself raw, that song. But it didn't matter. She turned away, and he knew she'd made her final choice. Just as well. He was so hurt, so full of blind rage, he wouldn't have been able to speak to her.

He saw *him*, Jeff, standing behind her. "Take care of her."

Jeff nodded, and Chase was satisfied. Even through the anger and searing pain, he wanted her to be happy, and it was clear Jeff made her happy.

The rest of the set flew by, and he collapsed in the green room, completely spent. He sipped water and settled in to wait for his band mates to finish partying with the rest of the festival bands. He wasn't up for a crowd, not then.

The door opened, and he started to bitch out the security guard, but the face he saw poking through the gap stopped his heart. She hesitated, unsure.

"You?" Chase's voice cracked into a whisper.

"I know you probably don't want to see me, of all people, but—"

"No, it's fine. Come on in." He set his bottle down and tried to gather his scattered wits. "What—uh, what are you doing here?"

She shrugged. "I don't know." She held up a backstage pass. "I have this...Anna—sorry, she gave it to me. So...here I am."

Her eyes held sorrow for him. That hurt, in an odd way. She cared about him? She saw his pain, clearly. "Here you are."

The silence stretched out, neither of them sure what to say, or do, or feel.

God, she's gorgeous. The thought struck him, unbidden.

For the first time in months, Anna was nowhere in his mind.

About the Author

JASINDA WILDER is a Michigan native with a penchant for titillating tales about sexy men and strong women. When she's not writing, she's probably shopping, baking, or reading. She loves to travel, and some of her favorite vacations spots are Las Vegas, New York City, and Toledo, Ohio. You can often find Jasinda drinking sweet red wine with frozen berries.

To find out more about Jasinda and her other titles, visit her website: www.Jasindawilder.com.

Made in the USA
Charleston, SC
02 February 2013